living a dream

richard roberts
shaun barrowes

Edited by
julie frederick

Copyright © 2025 by Rich's Creations

All rights reserved.

No part of this book may be reproduced in any form or by any electronic or mechanical means, including information storage and retrieval systems, without written permission from the author, except for the use of brief quotations in a book review.

Many thanks to my family for all their love and encouragement. To Shaun Barrowes for helping me pull this all together to make my dreams come true.

introduction

Dear Reader,

There is a THEME SONG that accompanies this book. The piano piece referenced in the book is a real song written and performed by Shaun Barrowes, and you can listen to here:

one

. . .

"HAVE you ever had a dream so real or a nightmare so vivid that you couldn't tell what was real?"

Wally Masters stared blankly at the living room's shag carpet beneath him, a battlefield of discarded beer bottles. The air was heavy with the sour stench of stale alcohol, but Wally didn't notice. He sat, slouched and unmoving, as though the couch had swallowed him whole. He had no idea how long he'd been there—hours? Days? Time had dissolved into something shapeless, more like how it passed in a dream than in reality.

The phone rang again, its shrill, piercing tone cutting through the oppressive silence. It was the fifth—maybe sixth—time today. Work, no doubt. His boss, coworkers, someone wondering why he hadn't shown up. The sound clawed at him, grating and relentless, but Wally couldn't move. The images and memories spinning in his mind held him captive, their pull stronger than the outside world. He stayed glued to his spot, staring at the TV in front of him, the screen's flickering images blending into a meaningless haze of colors and noise.

Outside, the sun was dipping low, its amber light filtering weakly through the blinds. The world beyond his living room was moving forward, but Wally was not. His mind swirled with a muddle of images, trapping him beneath their weight. He felt helpless, caught in the gravity of his own despair—like a man sinking into quicksand, too exhausted to fight.

A sudden knock shattered the stillness, loud and sharp, rattling the door. Wally's body flinched, but his mind barely stirred. The knock came again, more forceful this time, followed by a muffled voice calling his name. He ignored it. He was too absorbed in the vivid world inside his head—so consumed by the memories that his eyes couldn't truly see, and his body couldn't register the world around him.

The door flew open with a thunderous crash, slamming against the wall. Kevin stood in the doorway, breathless and wild-eyed, his face flushed. "Wally!" he shouted, his voice tight with panic. "Susan's been trying to reach you for three hours!"

Kevin's words barely registered. Wally's gaze drifted lazily past him, landing on the television again. He couldn't make sense of the urgency in Kevin's voice.

Kevin stormed across the room, his footsteps pounding against the floor. "Wally!" he repeated, his voice cracking now as he stopped just a few feet away. "It's Mikey—there was an accident!"

The words hung in the air, reverberating in the silence. Wally blinked slowly, his lips parting slightly, but no sound came out. He looked at Kevin, his eyes sliding over the face of the man he thought that he'd known for years, but his focus snagged on something small, something insignificant—the rough shadow of stubble lining Kevin's jaw. Kevin had always been clean-shaven, his face boyish and smooth, hadn't he?

Living A Dream

"Are you even listening to me?" Kevin's voice cracked as he lunged forward, grabbing Wally by the shoulders and shaking him hard. "Mikey! He's in the hospital! They don't know if he's going to make it!"

"Hospital?" Wally muttered the word foreign on his lips as he tried to grasp the meaning. Kevin pulled him to his feet. He stood slowly, his legs stiff, unable to process Kevin's presence in his living room.

Before he knew it, Kevin was gripping his arm with firm insistence and steering him toward the door. "Just get in the car. I'll drive," Kevin said, his voice clipped and urgent, already fumbling with his keys.

The next thing Wally knew, he was in the passenger seat of Kevin's 1967 Corvette Stingray, the engine roaring as they sped down Ritchie Highway. The hum of the car filled the space between them, but Wally barely noticed. His head rested against the window, the cool glass pressing against his forehead as the blur of trees and streetlights streaked past.

Wally cast a long glance at his friend. Kevin gripped the steering wheel tightly, his jaw set. Wally was trying to focus, trying to remember. He knew he cared—at least he had cared once—about Kevin, about Mikey, about Susan. But as he tried to remember, his focus slid away from the present and into the past. Fragments of memory surfaced, disjointed and hazy, like old photographs coming to life.

He had met Kevin the day after his dog died—that much he was sure of. But the details surrounding the death were a tangled mess, different, conflicting memories fighting for dominance. Wally squeezed his temples with trembling fingers, trying to make sense of them, blinking hard as though the motion would sharpen the images in his mind. He narrowed his eyes, willing himself to focus, to untangle the truth. His mind latched onto the first memory, pulling it forward from the haze.

. . .

Wally's father, Boyd Masters, leaned against the chipped kitchen counter, his dark gray coveralls streaked with oil and grease, the name *Western Electric* stitched over his chest like a badge of duty. A steaming mug of coffee rested in his calloused hands, his morning ritual. Outside the window, the quiet cul-de-sac of Aragorn Court was just beginning to stir. On hot summer days like this one, the hum of cicadas filled the air, mixing with the occasional rumble of a passing car on the distant highway. But on this late-August morning, the only sounds were the clink of Boyd's coffee mug and the soft creak of the linoleum as he shifted his weight.

Wally, just eight years old, sat a few feet away at the wooden table, quietly eating a bowl of cereal that had long since gone soggy. The floral-patterned vinyl tablecloth, slightly sticky from last night's dinner, clung to his bare arms as he hunched over his bowl. On rare Sunday mornings like this one, Boyd still had to work. He watched his father out of the corner of his eye, careful not to draw attention. Boyd wasn't the kind of man who made time for his kids—his presence loomed more like a shadow in their lives. But when it came to Lobo, their black labrador, Boyd's demeanor softened.

Everyone in the house knew it. Lobo meant more to Boyd than his own children ever had.

That's why it stood out when Boyd noticed something wasn't right with the dog. Lobo didn't greet him that morning with her usual wagging tail or eager jumps. She wasn't bounding around the small, fenced-in backyard, sniffing at the azalea bushes or chasing squirrels. Instead, she lay still on the kitchen floor, her eyes dull, her chest rising and falling with shallow, uneven breaths.

Boyd frowned, setting his coffee down with a clink and

crouching beside her. "Lobo?" he said gruffly, his voice low, almost tender. The dog gave a faint whimper, her body trembling, and then suddenly she heaved forward, vomiting violently on the linoleum. Her legs buckled as she collapsed, her body limp.

"Lobo! What's wrong, girl?" Boyd barked, his voice cracking with frustration as he laid a hand on her fur. "Tell me you didn't get into the rat poison!"

Wally froze in his chair, his spoon hovering in mid-air. He had overheard Boyd warning the neighbors just last week about setting out rat poison in their garages to deal with the vermin problem. Boyd had been adamant about keeping the dog away and had told Wally to watch her, but Wally hadn't thought much of it at the time. Now, panic bubbled up in his chest, cold and sharp, as he watched his father's face twist in anger.

Boyd's eyes darted to Wally, narrowing like a hawk's. He rose to his full height, his boots clomping heavily against the floor. In two long strides, he closed the distance, grabbing Wally by the front of his shirt and yanking him out of his chair. The cereal bowl clattered to the ground, milk spilling in a widening pool. Wally found himself nose to nose with his father, the sharp scent of coffee and sweat filling his nostrils.

"Boy," Boyd growled, his voice low and menacing. "I told you to keep Lobo away from the neighbors' rat poison, didn't I?" When Wally didn't answer, Boyd repeated, "Didn't I?"

Wally's breath hitched, his wide eyes fixed on his father's scowling face. His mouth opened, but no words came. His small body trembled as he braced for the inevitable slap or worse. But this time, it didn't come.

With a grunt, Boyd released him, shoving him back hard against the table. Without another word, Boyd scooped Lobo up into his arms, ignoring the vomit smeared on his coveralls. The dog whimpered weakly, her head lolling against his chest, and then Boyd was out the door, his heavy boots pounding against the wooden porch steps. The screen door slammed shut, and moments later, the roar of the truck engine echoed down the gravel driveway.

Wally stood frozen, the tension in his body refusing to release. The room fell silent, except for the faint drip of milk spilling off the edge of the table. For a fleeting moment, he thought he might be safe—until he turned and saw his brothers.

Roy and Tommy stood in the doorway, identical smirks curling their lips. Wally had managed to avoid them since yesterday's humiliation. They didn't care about Lobo or Boyd's anger. To them, this was just another opportunity.

"Where do you think you're going, squirt?" Roy sneered. "Couldn't even keep a dog safe."

"Yeah," Tommy added, "if anything happens to that dog, Dad'll come after you." Their laughter echoed off the walls as Wally bolted from the kitchen, his heart pounding.

"What a weakling!" Tommy wheezed between giggles.

"So pathetic," Roy added, his voice dripping with contempt.

Wally was big for his age but still much smaller than either of them. Most of the time, Roy and Tommy ignored him, tossing out passing remarks about his uselessness. But whenever they were bored or saw an opportunity, they loved to make his life miserable. That was their game—humiliate, hurt, repeat.

Just the day before, Tommy had pulled another one of his cruel pranks. Wally had stopped at a lemonade stand down the street, desperate for a cold drink in the sweltering summer heat. The girl running the stand was his age, maybe a year older, and Wally had been trying to work up the courage to talk to her. He'd carefully placed his coins on the table, his face red with nerves, and she had smiled politely as she poured him a cup. But just as he reached for it, Tommy appeared out of nowhere and yanked Wally's pants down to his ankles.

The shock froze him in place. He stood there in his underwear, his face burning as the girl gasped. The lemonade spilled onto the table and splattered onto the ground. Wally fumbled to pull his pants back up, but the damage was done.

Furious, he turned and charged at Tommy, his fists swinging wildly. He managed to land a punch to Tommy's side, but it didn't matter. Tommy, five years older and nearly twice his size, grabbed Wally with ease, pinning him to the ground. With a smirk, Tommy yanked his pants down again —this time taking his underwear too—and shoved him hard onto the pavement.

Wally had never felt so humiliated. His cheeks burned with shame as Tommy's laughter rang in his ears. His brothers loved tormenting him, especially in front of others. Pantsing him was one of their favorites, but they'd also clothesline him off his bike, steal his shoes, or shove him into puddles. It never stopped.

Hours later, Boyd returned home. Wally had been curled up in his room, replaying the morning in his head—worrying about what had happened to Lobo and what it might mean for him. He peeked out from his bedroom door as he heard the front door creak open. Boyd stepped inside, moving slowly, his face blank. Dangling from his hand was Lobo's collar, the worn leather strap swinging lifelessly as he shuffled into the kitchen. He didn't say a word. Wally quickly dashed back into his room and shut the door, hiding beneath his threadbare bed covers.

He hoped the covers would protect him, as though the thin fabric could shield him from the world outside.

They didn't.

The door flew open with a crash, and Boyd staggered inside. Heart pounding, Wally pulled the blankets over his head, praying the monster would pass him by. But a strong hand gripped his leg and yanked him out of bed, sending him crashing to the floor. He scrambled to get away, but Boyd's fist came down hard, knocking him back with a thud. Dizzy and disoriented, Wally barely had time to curl up before the first strike landed—sharp and searing across his back. The worn leather of Lobo's collar lashed down again and again, each blow leaving raw welts on his arms, legs, and shoulders as he tried to shield himself. The metal buckle bit into his skin, and Wally's throat burned from screaming.

The pain was overwhelming, and Wally teetered on the edge of blacking out. He had never taken such a beating. Boyd's slurred shouts filled the room, but through the chaos, Wally caught a few chilling words: "Lobo's gone, and it's all your fault, you miserable little cuss! Next time, why don't you do us all a favor and eat that rat poison yourself!"

Then his mother rushed in, her face twisted with fear. "Stop it!" she cried, grabbing Boyd's arm with a strength Wally had never seen in her. She pulled on him desperately, trying to drag him away from Wally.

Boyd turned on her, eyes wild and unfocused, the collar still clenched in his fist. With a snarl, he brought it down on her shoulder, the crack of leather against skin making her flinch. "I never should've let you have another kid!" he spat. "It's your fault he's worthless!"

Wally's mother cringed, backing out of the room, her eyes wide and pleading. "It's going to be okay," she stammered, her voice trembling. "We can get you another dog. Why don't you go have a drink with your friends? Go to the bar until you feel better," she begged, her words soft and placating.

"Never tell me what to do!" Boyd roared, swinging the collar at her again. She flinched, retreating instinctively, one arm raised defensively. For a moment, Boyd just glared at her, chest heaving. Then he staggered back, rage momentarily spent. Without another word, he stomped down the stairs and out of the house, the door slamming behind him with a thunderous thud.

Silence fell, heavy and suffocating. Wally lay motionless on the floor, every breath a struggle. The welts on his skin throbbed in time with his heartbeat. He knew the next few days would be a nightmare. All he could do was wish he could disappear—forever.

...

Kevin took a hard turn, jolting Wally against the car door and snapping him back to the present. Wally glanced at him, his thoughts a chaotic swirl as he tried to piece them together. He clearly remembered meeting Kevin the day after his dog died —that much was certain. But then another memory surfaced, sharp and unsettling: a different day, a different dog—a black labrador named Daisy.

...

Dad leaned against the polished kitchen counter, his white coat already on, his name stitched neatly above his heart. The bright morning sun streamed through the large bay window while the scent of maple syrup and freshly brewed coffee mingled in the air. Beyond the window, their quiet cul-de-sac in Hanover, Maryland, was coming to life. Wally could hear a few kids whizzing past on bicycles, their laughter drifting through the crisp morning air.

Dad was sipping his coffee, glancing over the day's schedule in his planner before heading to the hospital. Wally sat at the dining table, watching him, noting how focused he looked, even in these quiet moments. The soft hum of a kitchen radio played in the background—Frank Sinatra's voice crooning as Mom bustled around the stove.

Daisy seemed to sense Dad's departure, just as she always did. Their black lab padded over and rested her head against Dad's knee. His hand dropped instinctively to rub behind her ears, the way it always did, even when he was in a hurry.

Mom, wearing her white apron, had flour dusted on her hands as she flipped pancakes, the scent of warm batter filling the kitchen. Her laughter rang out when she turned to see Wally's older sister, Becky, with flour on her nose. Becky wrinkled her nose, pretending to be annoyed as Mom wiped her face with a damp cloth, but her eyes were laughing too. It was just another Tuesday morning in their quiet suburban home.

"Keep practicing those scales, okay, pal?" Dad said, kneeling down to Wally's level. He patted Wally with a reassuring hand before standing and making his way to the door. "I want to hear that new song when I get home," he called over his shoulder.

Wally nodded, grinning, already imagining himself at the upright piano in the den, his mother's patient voice guiding him through each note. Sensing his eagerness, she smiled. "There's thirty minutes before school. You have a little time if you'd like to—" but before she could finish, Wally bolted from the kitchen, his socked feet skidding slightly on the hardwood floors as he raced to the piano to plunk out *The Entertainer* by Scott Joplin a few more times.

That afternoon, after school, Wally was in the backyard, kicking a soccer ball against the wooden fence, the rhythmic thud filling the air. Daisy ran after the ball each time, barking excitedly, her tail wagging as she bounded from one side of the yard to the other. The golden sunlight filtered through the tall oaks lining the property, casting long shadows across the grass.

Wally laughed, kicking the ball over and over. He had set up two orange cones at the far end of the yard, pretending they were goalposts. His sneakers scuffed against the brick patio, leaving faint dust marks as he chased after Daisy, who playfully dodged around him.

However, his next kick sent the ball sailing over the hedge, bouncing into the quiet street beyond. Before Wally could run to catch her, Daisy darted after it, her paws skimming the grass, her eyes locked on the ball.

"Daisy, no!" Wally screamed, his heart slamming against his ribs.

The sound of an oncoming pickup truck rumbled in the distance. There was a sharp squeal of tires, a loud slam, followed by a yelp—then silence.

Wally felt rooted to the spot, his legs unwilling to carry him forward, as if moving would make it real. The chirping cicadas suddenly felt deafening, the world narrowing to a single moment.

When he finally found himself standing over Daisy, he saw her familiar, gentle face—now still. Her eyes were closed, her fur ruffled by the evening breeze. The world seemed to go silent around him, the only sound the rapid thudding of his own heart.

The rest of that afternoon was a blur—his mother's arms wrapping around him, her soft voice breaking as she called for Dad. Wally's father's steady hands and voice, low and calm, said things Wally couldn't quite hear. Becky appeared beside him, her hand slipping over his shoulder, comforting him.

They buried Daisy that evening in a corner of the backyard beneath the old maple tree. Dad had insisted on digging the grave himself, his jaw set, his eyes bright with unshed tears as he worked. Wally sat with Becky and his mother on the grass, his hands clutched around a worn soccer ball, the last one he'd kicked for Daisy.

When the grave was ready, they each placed something beside her—a stick from Wally, one of Becky's old hair ribbons, Mom's handkerchief. Dad reached into his pocket and pulled out a tennis ball he would often throw when playing fetch with Daisy. He didn't say anything, just placed it down gently, his hands lingering there for a moment.

They stood together, arms wrapped around each other, the late evening light casting long shadows across the grass. No one spoke. Wally could feel his father's hand resting heavy on his shoulder, his mother's fingers woven through his own. In that stillness, with the world closing in around them, they shared the heavy loss. Together.

When they returned to the house, Wally couldn't help but notice how quiet and empty it now felt. That night, Wally couldn't sleep. He lay awake, staring at the ceiling, hearing phantom sounds of Daisy's paws padding down the hall, the soft jingle of her collar.

Dad came in after a while, sitting down at the edge of Wally's bed. He didn't say anything, just reached over and brushed a hand through Wally's hair, his touch steady and comforting. Wally turned toward him, the tears he'd been holding back all evening finally spilling over.

"I didn't mean for him to—" Wally's voice broke, and Dad shook his head, his hand resting firm on Wally's shoulder.

"It wasn't your fault, pal," he said quietly. "Sometimes things happen, even when we try our best." He took a shaky breath, his own eyes glistening. "Death is a part of life. What matters is what we do with the time we've been given."

They sat together in silence, and for the first time, Wally saw his father's own grief, felt the weight of it in the way Dad's hand lingered on his shoulder, in the quiet tremor of his voice.

As he tucked Wally in and turned to leave, Wally called out, his voice small. "Dad?"

His father paused in the doorway, glancing back.

"Do you think we'll ever see Daisy again?" Wally whispered.

Dad nodded, a sad smile pulling at the corners of his mouth. "I hope so, pal."

As the house finally fell into silence, Wally cried himself to sleep, knowing he would wake up in the morning with that empty feeling, knowing Daisy was still gone, and it was all his fault.

...

Kevin slammed on the brakes, the tires screeching as a car veered recklessly in front of them, cutting across lanes to make a left turn from the right. The jolt snapped Wally back to the present, his body lurching forward before the seatbelt caught him. He glanced at Kevin, who muttered a curse under his breath, his grip tightening on the wheel. Wally frowned, taken aback—he didn't think he could recall ever seeing his best friend this tense, this visibly upset. For a moment, he simply stared, bewildered, as Kevin's jaw clenched and his knuckles whitened. But the moment passed quickly, and Wally's mind slipped back into the past, drifting once again to his conflicting memories. Both felt vivid, both felt real, but only one could be the real story. Which one was true? The question buzzed in his mind, making him feel lightheaded, the world spinning at an uneven tilt as he struggled to sort through two conflicting memories.

It was Lobo and the rat poison. He was sure of it. Or was he? He could still smell the fresh-cut grass from the day Daisy bolted into the street. In one version, it was Lobo who died— tied to memories of an angry, abusive family that left Wally too numb to care. In the other, it was Daisy, his black lab, part of a loving, supportive household. Daisy's death brought real grief—a sadness that echoed the bond they'd shared. Lobo's death brought pain, bruises, and even more hatred from his father. Two opposing realities tugged at him, each vivid and haunting, yet impossibly at odds.

Wally squeezed his eyes shut. The memories overlapped—rat poison, the street. They blurred together, slipping between past and present.

two
. . .

WALLY LOOKED OVER AT KEVIN, who was speeding down the road. Something else was more important than how his dog had died. What was it? Wally struggled to focus on the present as the memories collided and slid over each other. Kevin glanced at him, his eyes full of sympathy and worry—a look Wally knew all too well.

...

It was that next day, in the bustling school cafeteria, as he sat lost in thought, a skinny boy with a neatly tucked-in shirt sat down next to him. He pushed his glasses up the bridge of his nose and extended his hand.

"I'm Kevin," he said, sticking out his hand. "Nice to meet you."

Wally whipped his head around, scowling. Kevin had never talked to him before or tried to sit nearby, and Wally preferred it that way. Kevin kept his hand out for a few seconds before slowly pulling it back, sensing Wally wasn't in

Living A Dream

the mood to make friends. Undeterred, he studied Wally for a moment before reaching into his backpack and pulling out a brand-new issue of *The Flash*.

Everyone in class knew Kevin was the nerdiest kid in third grade. Wally really didn't want to be seen with him. Everyone would think he was a nerd, too. "I don't want to read your comics!" Wally said with a subtle shake of the head. He hoped nobody saw their interaction.

Kevin flinched but quietly put the comic back. He glanced at Wally a few more times throughout class as if trying to figure out why he was so closed off. They sat in silence for the rest of class, but Wally could feel Kevin's curious eyes on him.

"Why are you staring at me?" Wally asked, raising an eyebrow.

"I'm sorry," Kevin said. "You just looked like you could use a friend."

Wally didn't respond, eyeing the boy curiously.

On their way to recess, Wally was about to make a break for the playground when he caught sight of Kevin getting pushed around by two fourth graders.

"You're such a nerd, Kevin!" one of them sneered, grabbing his bag and shoving him into the lockers. They pulled out his comic book and waved it around. "Look at this dope! If I ever saw anyone wearing red tights like this, I'd give 'em a knuckle sandwich."

Before Wally could think, something came over him—maybe it was the memory of feeling helpless as his dog died and the pain that followed. Without hesitation, he charged at the boys, shoving one hard enough to send him sprawling to the floor. He followed up with a swift punch to the other boy's gut, doubling him over with a grunt. Wally might only have been in third grade, but he was big for his age, and all that pent-up anger and bitterness made him stronger than he seemed.

"Masters? What's your deal?" the boy on the floor yelled.

"Leave him alone!" Wally snapped, his fists clenched. The other boy shrunk under Wally's glare, helping his friend up as they scurried off.

Kevin picked up his comic and slipped it back into his bag. "Thanks, but you didn't have to do that."

Wally shrugged. "Maybe if you weren't such a nerd, they wouldn't mess with you."

Kevin smiled softly. "I like what I like."

The next day, Kevin sat next to Wally again. This time, he pulled out an *Archie* comic. Wally had seen some of the older kids reading those, laughing at the goofy stories. They weren't as nerdy as most comics he had seen Kevin holding. Even some of the popular kids read *Archie*.

Kevin seemed to notice Wally's interest. "You wanna read it?"

Wally, without thinking, nodded. Kevin grinned and handed it to him. Wally grabbed it and spent the first ten minutes of class sneaking peeks, stifling a few chuckles as the teacher glared at him. The stories were a welcome distraction, helping him forget—if only for a little while—how hard it was going to be to go home.

When the bell rang, Wally handed it back. "That wasn't so bad. I actually enjoyed reading it."

"I can bring more tomorrow," Kevin offered, his face lighting up.

Wally nodded slowly, hesitant to commit. The last thing he wanted was for Kevin to think they were friends.

True to his word, Kevin brought a stack of *Archie* comics the next day. "You have that many?" Wally asked, eyes wide in surprise.

Kevin chuckled. "I've got way more at home."

"You really are a nerd," Wally said, but this time with a smile.

Throughout class, Wally snuck glances at the comics,

stifling laughs and occasionally nudging Kevin to share what he found funny.

At lunch, Wally found himself absorbed in the humor of Archie, Jughead, and Blondie. Every time he showed Kevin a funny page, Kevin would laugh and point out one of his own favorites. Despite himself, Wally realized he was actually enjoying Kevin's company.

By the end of the week, he'd gone through at least fifty comics, managing to remain mostly undetected by their teachers. On Friday, Kevin invited Wally to his house for dinner. Wally hesitated—it felt like a step toward a friendship he wasn't sure he wanted. But after enjoying their time together all week, he agreed.

They spent the afternoon talking and reading comics, the soft notes of the piano drifting in from the living room where Kevin's mom played. Wally paused mid-page to listen, the melody winding through the quiet house. Kevin seemed to notice.

"She always plays at night, just before dinner," Kevin said with a shrug, almost rolling his eyes.

Wally nodded, still listening. "It's nice."

"She makes me practice every day," Kevin added, but his voice softened, betraying a hint of appreciation. Both of them fell silent, letting the heart-wrenching melodies carry them away.

When Kevin's favorite show, *Dr. Kildare,* came on, his mom stopped playing to let them watch it together. Wally had never seen it before, but it didn't take long for it to become his favorite, too.

...

. . .

The car screeched to a stop in front of Anne Arundel General. Kevin, now in his mid-twenties, quickly circled around and yanked open the passenger door, half-dragging Wally out. Wally stumbled but managed to straighten, his body struggling to find its footing on the entryway while his mind reeled, still trying to catch up.

Inside, Kevin had a hurried conversation with a pair of nurses while Wally stared down the hallway leading to the hospital rooms. He knew these halls, didn't he? He knew every step of them. The nurses silently pointed them toward Mikey's room.

As they entered the sterile corridors, Wally's body moved instinctively, going through the motions. Despite the fog clouding his mind and the blurred line between reality and dreams, he navigated the hospital with practiced ease—like his muscles remembered what his mind couldn't. The hundreds of hours he'd spent here during med classes, shadowing, and studying seemed to have left an imprint on him, guiding his steps.

The lights buzzed softly overhead, the faint scent of antiseptic hanging in the air—a backdrop so familiar it seemed to guide him, even as it also felt disjointed and unreal. His steps quickened, his shoulders squared. Without fully realizing it, he slipped into doctor mode, his movements steady and purposeful, as though Mikey were just another patient waiting for him.

Then he stepped into the hospital room.

The sight of Mikey stopped him cold.

His little boy—his six-year-old son—lay motionless on the hospital bed, his chest rising and falling with labored breaths. A web of IV lines snaked around him, monitors beeping out a rhythm that sent ice through Wally's veins. Mikey let out a faint groan, his small hand twitching against the sheets, clutching his chest.

Wally inhaled sharply, his throat tightening. His legs

Living A Dream

locked, his body momentarily forgetting how to move. He had seen this before—the fragile, too-pale skin, the way a small body seemed swallowed up by a hospital bed. He didn't think he could bear seeing Mikey like this. His heart was already breaking.

But his professional mind knew that none of those feelings would help. Forcing the grief aside, Wally's instincts took over, assessing injuries and slipping into doctor mode. He turned to the attending physician, his voice strained but steady.

"What do we have here, doctor?" he asked, the words coming out firm, carrying the authority of a seasoned surgeon. But even as he spoke, his eyes never left his son.

The attending doctor flicked his gaze to Wally, then back to Mikey, shining a light in the boy's eyes while the X-rays glowed ominously on the wall.

Behind him, Susan let out a sharp breath. "Why haven't you been answering your damn phone?" Her voice cracked with restrained fury. A bandage cut across her forehead, and her right wrist was wrapped in a brace.

Wally flinched at the sound of Susan's voice, a jumble of memories surging up, his mind struggling to organize them into something coherent. He tried to connect Susan's words to what he was seeing, but everything felt disjointed and out of focus.

"We were hit by another car!" she spat.

Wally blinked. His eyes darted to the X-rays, then back to his son.

Hit by a car.

The words slammed into him, rearranging everything in an instant.

Mikey. His son. In a car accident.

He should be at his side. He should be holding his hand, telling him that he was there, that Daddy would fix everything. But his body was still locked between instinct and emotion, between doctor and father.

"When did it happen?" Wally asked, his voice slipping into something clinical, detached, even as his stomach roiled.

"Approximately three hours ago," the doctor answered.

Susan's glare burned into him. "That's all you have to say?" Her voice trembled, her hands curled into fists. "Don't you care that your own son might be dyi—" She choked on the word, unable to finish.

Wally's jaw clenched. Care? If she only knew the war raging inside him, the fight between his doctor's discipline and the desperate need to collapse at Mikey's bedside. But emotions wouldn't save his son. Focus would.

His gaze snapped to the X-rays, his mind latching onto the only thing he knew how to control—the diagnosis. He analyzed the images with razor-sharp precision, his brain shifting into high gear. He noted every detail—the shallow rise and fall of Mikey's chest, the pale tint of his skin—and compared it to what he saw on the film. His mind raced, piecing together the clues. Finally, he spoke, his voice calm but firm, with a quiet authority that cut through the tension in the room.

"Doctor, that looks like a diaphragmatic hernia. He needs surgery—now."

Susan turned to him sharply, her brow furrowed.

The doctor hesitated, his eyes sweeping over Wally's disheveled appearance. "Oh, so you're also a doctor?" His tone was skeptical, his nose twitching as he caught the faint scent of alcohol on Wally's breath.

"Yes," Wally replied automatically, his focus unwavering.

Susan continued to stare at him, her expression a mix of shock and anger.

Wally pointed to the X-ray, his fingers tracing a shadowy outline only he seemed to notice. "Look here," he said, locking eyes with the doctor. "The left hemidiaphragm—it's elevated. You can see the bowel loops herniating into the thoracic cavity. That's not normal, especially after blunt force trauma from a car accident."

He continued, his tone more authoritative. "The mediastinum is slightly shifted to the right." He gestured. "Do you see this?"

The doctor raised an eyebrow but leaned closer, examining the X-rays with him.

"The mediastinum is shifting to the right. That's pressure building from the abdominal organs pushing into the chest. He's not just in pain—he's losing oxygen, fast." Wally paused, glancing back at Susan. "If you wait much longer, there's going to be tension in the lungs and heart."

The doctor, now fully engaged, studied the X-rays beside Wally, nodding. "Yes, I see it."

Something about Wally's insistence clearly unsettled him. "We're short on staff today. There's only one pediatric surgeon, and he's tied up in another operation," the doctor admitted.

"Well, get him out!" Wally demanded. "If you don't..." His unspoken warning hung heavy in the room.

The doctor exchanged a glance with the nurse before nodding. "I'll do what I can."

The moment the doctor left, the weight of it all crashed into Wally.

His body moved before his mind could catch up, carrying him around to the other side of Mikey's bed, opposite Susan. His knees hit the floor as he reached for Mikey's hand. It was small. Too small. Warm, but limp.

A tremor ran through Wally's fingers as he smoothed a damp strand of hair from his son's forehead. "Mikey," he whispered, his voice hoarse. "I'm here, buddy. Daddy's here." His throat burned, his chest tightening like a vise.

From the other side of the bed, Susan shifted in her chair, her body stiff. Wally instinctively glanced at her, searching for some shared acknowledgment of the crushing moment, but she turned away, her posture rigid.

She didn't speak. She didn't even look at him.

Wally swallowed hard, staying on his knees beside Mikey's bed, the weight of Susan's silence pressing heavily on him. His head began to spin, competing memories resurfacing in a chaotic blur as he tried to understand why Susan was so upset with him. He struggled to focus on the details, but the door burst open, and two nurses strode in with grim efficiency.

"Excuse us," one said briskly, already moving to disconnect the monitors.

Wally blinked, disoriented. "What are you—"

"He's being prepped for surgery," the other nurse cut in, her voice firm but not unkind.

Wally nodded mutely, his voice swallowed by the lump in his throat. He remained rooted to the spot as the nurses transferred Mikey onto a mobile bed and wheeled him swiftly out. The rhythmic squeak of the rolling wheels faded into the hallway, leaving behind an aching silence.

As the last nurse exited, the room seemed to grow heavier, the emptiness pressing in around him. Wally tore his gaze from the doorway and turned to Susan. She was staring at him, brow furrowed in confusion, her eyes searching his face for something she couldn't seem to find. For a brief moment, it looked like she might say something—but then, without a word, she stood abruptly. Her steps were quick and determined, carrying her toward the hallway to likely update her parents, who were waiting in the lounge with Kevin.

Before the door swung shut, Wally caught the clipped edge of her voice, low but sharp:

"I don't even know who that man is in there. Whoever he is, he isn't my hus—"

The door closed, cutting off the rest.

Wally stood motionless, the echo of her words sinking into

his chest like lead. When his gaze drifted to the mirror, he froze. The man staring back at him was a stranger—hollow eyes, disheveled hair, and a face that looked like it had been dragged through the gutter. He barely recognized himself. But the longer he stared, the more another face emerged from the reflection.

His father. The man who loved Lobo more than him. Who drank himself into rages and beat Wally more times than he could count. The thought sent a cold shiver through him.

But then the other memory surfaced—his father, the doctor, coming home late, weary and exhausted from twelve-hour shifts in surgery, saving lives. The man who draped an arm over Wally when Daisy died, gently explaining that death was just a part of life.

He looked like both. The memories overlapped, their edges blurred, leaving Wally standing in a fog of contradictions.

His chest tightened.

Was that what Susan was seeing? Could she sense the fractures inside him? Both memories were so clear, so real. Accepting that one wasn't real would mean admitting that the other couldn't be either. What was happening to his world? Even with his son in the hospital, he couldn't tell what was real anymore.

With the blinds pulled up, Wally could see through the large window into the hallway, where Susan stood with her parents. They greeted her with worried expressions, their postures heavy with unspoken fear. A nurse gently redirected them to a waiting area just across the hall, where they sank into the stiff chairs, their bodies tense, bracing for whatever news would come next.

Wally let out a slow breath and lowered himself into the chair beside Mikey's now-empty bed. For a long moment, he simply stared at the faint impression in the mattress—the only proof that his son had been there at all. His gaze shifted to the window, back to Susan. Her parents flanked her like sentinels while she sat with her face buried in her hands. They whispered words he couldn't hear, their gestures small but comforting. But Susan barely moved.

Her shoulders trembled slightly.

A sharp pang shot through Wally's chest.

And then, without warning, a memory surfaced—Susan's laugh, bright and unguarded, from the day they first met.

How long ago had that been?

Years. A lifetime, it seemed now.

Back then, her smile had been effortless, her eyes filled with the kind of fire that had drawn him in like a moth to a flame.

Wally swallowed hard, unable to look away from her as his mind drifted back to the day they first met—the first day of junior year.

...

three

. . .

BY THE TIME their junior year rolled around, both Wally and Kevin were feeling more confident. With Wally's older brothers out of the house and long gone, he no longer had to keep a wary eye out for their pranks. Not like that first day of ninth grade, when Tommy gave him a ride to school only to pants him at the front entrance. It took Wally the rest of the year to live that down.

Kevin was eager to dive back into math club competitions and tournaments, ready to prove himself as a top contender, while Wally felt a surge of anticipation as he prepared to compete for a first-string position on the varsity football team.

They made their way to their first class—Biology. Over the summer, they had aligned their schedules to share most of their classes, including an elective: a music class that gave both Kevin and Wally a creative outlet to explore their shared passion.

As they walked, Wally's eyes were constantly scanning the hallway, lingering on every girl they passed. A few smiled back, causing his cheeks to flush slightly. He was tall and lean and stood out in a good way, but he never quite knew what to say to girls. Both he and Kevin had vowed to change that and get a girlfriend by the end of the year.

In Biology, Wally insisted they sit in the back. "Better view," he said with a grin, sweeping his hand across the room as if sizing up their classmates. Kevin didn't protest, and they took seats in the last row.

As the class filled up, their teacher, standing in front of a large blackboard, began writing his name in big chalk letters. The well-worn hardwood floors creaked as students shuffled to their desks, and by the time the bell rang, almost every seat was filled. Then, just as class was about to begin, the last student rushed in—a new girl they had never seen before. Wally's heart nearly stopped.

She was the most beautiful girl he'd ever seen.

"Who's that?" Wally whispered to Kevin, barely able to contain his excitement.

Kevin shrugged. "How should I know?"

The girl was petite, with a high, golden blonde ponytail tied with a soft pink ribbon. The ends of her hair flipped outward perfectly, bouncing with every step. She wore a sleeveless A-line dress that ended just above her knees, her appearance effortlessly stylish. She took the last open seat at the front of the room, and the teacher seemed pleased to have her sitting right in front of him.

As the teacher launched into an introduction to Biology, Wally barely heard a word. His eyes kept drifting back to the girl, unable to focus on anything else. At one point, she must have felt eyes on the back of her head because she turned around suddenly and locked eyes with him for a brief second before he quickly looked away, his face burning.

The final minutes of class felt like an eternity. Wally's palms grew sweaty as he thought about talking to her after the bell. He wasn't sure he could muster the courage. When the bell finally rang, he froze, still sitting at his desk, paralyzed with indecision. Kevin, noticing his tight grip on the desk, smirked.

"You okay, pal?" Kevin asked.

"Huh?" Wally released his death grip. "Yeah, I'm good."

Kevin leaned in with a grin. "This wouldn't have anything to do with that blonde girl up front, would it?"

Wally's eyes widened. "Shh! Are you nuts? She'll hear you!"

The girl gathered her things and walked out into the hallway, disappearing around the corner. As soon as she was gone, Wally smacked Kevin's arm.

"I'm gonna talk to her," Wally said, standing up with sudden determination.

"Right now?" Kevin's eyebrows shot up. "You're just gonna walk up to her? What are you gonna say?"

"I don't know. Maybe, 'How ya doin'?" Wally replied, casually rolling up the sleeve of his plain white t-shirt. Thanks to the jobs they worked over the summer, they had finally been able to buy their own clothes. Wally had picked up a few pairs of straight-leg Levi 501s, a couple of crewneck sweaters, and a stack of crisp white t-shirts that felt effortlessly cool. But his favorite purchase by far was a pair of Converse sneakers he'd saved for and bought just before school started.

Despite Wally's best efforts to help Kevin upgrade his style, Kevin stubbornly stuck to khakis and button-down shirts, claiming they were "classic." Still, Wally managed to convince him to step a little outside his comfort zone with his first pair of Converse, though he insisted on a neutral color to "keep it practical."

Kevin scoffed. "*How ya doin'?* That's your big line? You can't just walk up to a girl like her and say, *how ya doin'!*"

"Sure I can. Just watch," Wally said, grabbing his bag. He made a beeline for the hallway, Kevin hurrying behind him. They stepped into the bustling corridor, but she was nowhere to be found. Wally glanced around, trying to play it cool. "I'll catch her next time," he said, forcing a casual shrug.

"Whatever you say, pal," Kevin said with a chuckle.

"What? I mean it!" Wally insisted.

"Mm-hmm," Kevin responded.

Their next class was P.E., and to Wally's delight, the blonde girl from Biology was there. They called roll, and Wally learned her name—Susan. Susan stood on the gym floor, bouncing lightly on her feet in fresh, white gym clothes. Wally almost tripped over himself staring at her, and if Kevin hadn't yanked him by the arm, he might have embarrassed himself in front of the whole class.

The gym teacher had set up an obstacle course that included a rope climb, a medicine ball toss, and a push-up station. Wally threw himself into each challenge, trying to impress Susan, even if she wasn't watching. He excelled at almost everything, while Kevin struggled to keep pace but managed not to fall too far behind.

While Wally was cranking out push-ups, he noticed her glance his way. Seizing the moment, he threw one arm behind his back and started doing one-armed push-ups, hoping to catch her attention. Their eyes met, and he swore he saw a hint of a smile.

Later, during the rope climb, Wally decided to show off even more. He stuck his legs out and climbed using only his arms, earning a few more glances. From the bottom of the rope, Kevin mumbled, "Show off." Wally caught another look from Susan, so he flexed and added a pull-up at the top for good measure before sliding back down.

After gym class, Kevin and Wally changed in the locker room. "Did you see that, Kev? I got her attention. Twice!"

"Oh, I saw alright," Kevin said, adjusting his glasses. "The whole class saw you making a fool of yourself."

"She likes me. I can tell," Wally said, leaning back against the wall, hands behind his head, grinning.

"Get real, pal," Kevin said, snapping a towel at Wally's thigh. "She doesn't even know your name."

Wally leaned forward and slung an arm around his friend. "She will soon. You can bet on it!"

...

The door opened, pulling him back to the present. Wally looked up from Mikey's empty hospital bed to see Kevin entering the room.

"The nurses couldn't give me any more information. How are you doing?" Kevin asked.

"I'm alright," Wally responded automatically. "I learned everything I needed from the X-rays."

Kevin raised an eyebrow. "The X-rays?" he repeated. "What's going on, Wally? You haven't seemed cognizant since I dragged you out of your apartment."

Wally opened his mouth to respond, to explain, but the memories were still swirling—vivid and relentless. He stared at Kevin, his throat tight, frustration building beneath the confusion. He knew he needed to stay in the present, to focus on Mikey, but his mind kept dragging him back.

Kevin stared back, a flicker of concern in his eyes, then sighed. "I have to go, but I'll check on you later."

Wally just nodded numbly, watching Kevin leave. He was sure now that he remembered Kevin... and Susan. Those two were part of all the memories, weren't they?

But before he could sort it out, his mind pulled him right back into another memory.

...

. . .

The next day in P.E., Wally was back at it, laying it on thick, hoping to catch Susan's attention. He threw himself into every drill, trying to show off, but no matter what he did, she didn't glance his way. By the end of class, as the bell rang, Wally was frustrated. For the rest of the week, he tried a few more things —laughing too loud with Kevin, catching a football directly in front of her—but nothing worked. She was always surrounded by her group of friends, making it impossible to get near her.

"I don't get it," Wally muttered to Kevin during lunch. "It worked the first time."

Kevin shook his head, smirking. "Maybe because the first time, you didn't look like you were trying so hard."

"You think that's it?" Wally said.

"Actually, no, you definitely looked like you were trying hard on Monday, too," Kevin said with a scoff.

"What? You think you could do better?" Wally shot back.

"No way, pal. I'm not as eager as you are to fall flat on my face," Kevin said, raising his eyebrows.

"Very funny," Wally grumbled, giving Kevin a playful shove.

Just before the school year began, Wally had impressed the coaches during football tryouts, earning a spot as the starting free safety and third-string quarterback on the varsity team. A late-summer growth spurt had worked to his advantage, adding both height and muscle to his frame. Still, it wasn't enough to challenge the team's senior quarterbacks, Johnny Wilds and Jimmy Bates. Johnny, the first-string quarterback, reveled in his status. Strutting through the halls in his letterman jacket, he never missed an opportunity to flaunt his position, always surrounded by his loyal entourage.

Now, on the football field during practice, Wally's mind wandered. His attention drifted to the far side of the field, where Susan stood with her cheer squad. Her bright red and white uniform practically shimmered in the afternoon sun, and she moved with effortless grace, her ponytail bouncing as she laughed with her teammates. Wally stared longer than he meant to, his thoughts unraveling into daydreams, until the sharp sting of a football smacking against his helmet jolted him back to reality.

"Quit gawking at the cheerleaders and get your head in the game, Masters!" Johnny's voice barked across the field, dripping with mockery. Laughter rippled through the players, and Wally's face burned as he scrambled to refocus.

Wally jumped back into their drills, but he couldn't help sneaking a few more glances at Susan. During a break, their eyes finally met for the briefest of moments, and Wally felt a spark of excitement. As if on cue, another football sailed toward him, and this time, he caught it just in time.

After practice, Wally paced nervously along the field, trying to psych himself up. "It's now or never," he muttered to himself. Taking a deep breath, he started the long, nerve-wracking walk toward Susan, who was busy putting away pom-poms on the side of the field.

By the time he reached her, he was out of breath. "Uh, hi—this your first day of practice?" he blurted out before he could stop himself.

Startled, Susan stood up, looking at him curiously. After a beat, she smiled politely. "Oh, you. The rope climber from P.E."

"Uh, yeah, that's me."

"We started practices last week."

"Oh... groovy. Were you a cheerleader at your last school?" Wally asked, desperate to keep the conversation going.

"No, I almost didn't try out this year. My friend talked me into it," she said.

"Well, you're a natural," Wally said, hoping it didn't sound too rehearsed. "The squad's lucky to have you."

"I wouldn't say that," she replied with a small laugh. "After today, they probably regret putting me on the squad."

Wally grinned. "I seriously doubt that." He shifted nervously. "I'm Wally, by the way."

"Susan," she said, offering her hand.

"My buddy Kev and I were thinking of grabbing a cola at Reads right now. Wanna join us?" Wally asked, trying to sound casual.

Susan's face lit up. "Reads? They have good shakes!"

Before Wally could get too excited, Johnny Wilds walked up and threw his arm around Susan's shoulders, pulling her close. "You trying to steal my girl, Masters?" he asked, smirking as he kissed the top of Susan's head.

Wally's heart sank, but he did his best to hide his disappointment. "Oh, you're already…" his voice trailed off.

As if reading his mind, Johnny answered, "I met this little honey over the summer while working as a lifeguard at North Shore. She fell for me instantly." He said with a wink. She elbowed him playfully.

Wally's mind raced for a quick exit when Kevin suddenly appeared by his side, seemingly out of nowhere. "Hey, pal, we gotta jet," Kevin said, casually saving the day.

Wally, grateful for the lifeline, forced a shrug. "It was nice meeting you, Susan."

He met Johnny's gaze for a moment, then turned to follow Kevin off the field. Once they were out of earshot, Kevin chuckled. "I can't believe you just walked up to her and talked to her."

"Me neither," Wally said, still trying to process it. He threw an arm around Kevin, slapping him on the back. "I don't know what got into me."

"You got some gumption, pal," Kevin said with a grin. "Now let's hit Reads and see if they've got the latest issue of *The Flash*."

Living A Dream

"You really love that one, don't you?" Wally teased, shaking his head. "*Batman* is so much better!"

"Aw, come on, you just haven't given *The Flash* a fair shake," Kevin replied, eyes lighting up. "The last issue left off on a doozy of a cliffhanger."

They headed to Reads Drugstore, grabbing bottles of Coca-Cola at the counter before drifting toward the comic book racks. Kevin immediately found the latest *Flash* issue and eagerly flipped it open, pointing out his favorite panels to Wally. But Wally barely listened, his thoughts fully devoted to the conversation he had had with Susan just moments earlier. His eyes darted toward the door as if hoping she might change her mind and meet them there.

As if his dream suddenly manifested itself, Wally couldn't believe his eyes when Susan walked through the door. He double blinked, wondering if he was seeing things. And then, to his horror, Johnny and half the football team followed. Panic shot through Wally. He spun around and ducked behind the shelf, heart pounding.

"Masters?" Johnny's voice boomed from the doorway. Wally reluctantly straightened up, finding every eye on him, including Susan's.

"Uh, hey, fellas. Just grabbing the latest *Archie*," Wally muttered, awkwardly holding up the issue he'd grabbed.

"You're hanging out in the comic book section, huh, Masters?" Johnny called out, a smirk playing on his lips as a few of his friends snickered.

Before Wally could think of a response, Johnny and the rest had already turned their attention to the diner counter, ordering milkshakes without a second thought. Wally cursed under his breath.

"What's wrong, pal?" Kevin asked, eyeing his friend.

"We are, that's what," Wally grumbled. "Now Susan's gonna think I'm a complete square."

Kevin shrugged. "What's wrong with that?" he said, eyes still on his comics.

Wally sighed and peeked over the shelves. Susan was sipping a malt milkshake, sitting next to Johnny at the counter. The boys were loud, laughing, and shoving each other while Susan sat quietly, barely entertained. Nobody was even noticing her.

Wally felt a pull to slide into the empty seat beside her, but the confidence he once had crossing the football field seemed to vanish. Instead, he sank to the floor, burying himself in an *Archie* comic, hoping the crowd would clear out soon.

"Should we go?" Kevin asked, holding a stack of comics. "You want that one?"

"Yeah, let's make it snappy." Wally stood, glancing nervously at the football players, who were now finishing their milkshakes. The diner counter was right next to the register—there was no avoiding them. "Here, let me take those," he offered, grabbing the stack of comics and holding them close to his side, trying to shield them from view.

It didn't work.

"Hey, Masters! Whatcha got there?" Johnny shot up from his seat and trotted over. Before Wally could react, Johnny snatched the comics out of his hand. "*The Flash*? *Batman*? Some other joker in tights? Geez, Masters, I didn't peg you for a full-on egghead." He laughed, loud enough for his friends to join in, their chuckles echoing through the store. A few of them crowded around, peeking over Johnny's shoulder as he flipped through the comics. "So, this is what gets you going, huh? Guys in tights? Whatever blows your hair back, I guess. Some of us are more into dames." He laughed again as Kevin quietly pushed through the crowd to pay for the comics.

The lady at the register handed Kevin his change, and the two bolted out of Reads. Wally felt deflated, humiliated in front of the entire football team—and worse, in front of Susan.

"Shake it off, pal," Kevin said. "Those deadbeats don't

know what they're talking about."

Wally sighed as he slid into the passenger seat of Kevin's Ford Falcon, the familiar squeak of the door hinges cutting through the quiet afternoon. As they headed back to Kevin's house, the warm autumn air streamed through the open windows, rustling Wally's hair. He stared out at the passing streets, his thoughts swirling. His exchanges with Susan and Johnny replayed in his mind like a broken record. It didn't help that Johnny Wilds seemed to have everything Wally didn't—a senior with a letterman jacket, brimming with confidence and charisma, always surrounded by a loyal crowd of followers. How was Wally supposed to compete with that?

Beside him, Kevin rattled on enthusiastically about the latest *Flash* comic, his words filling the small car with energy. But Wally barely heard him. He remained quiet, lost in his own world, staring out at the horizon as he turned over ways to salvage his reputation.

In the weeks that followed, Wally poured himself into football, seizing every opportunity to stand out, to impress, to prove he belonged. He played with a fire that made coaches nod in approval and teammates take notice. But as safety, he was stuck in the shadows. The glory belonged to quarterbacks, wide receivers—players whose names filled the morning announcements. If he wanted Susan to notice him, tackles wouldn't be enough. He needed the spotlight.

So, he set his sights on Johnny Wilds' position. He stayed after practice, working on his spiral until his fingers ached. He studied plays long after the others had gone home. He was determined.

Johnny, of course, never trained alone. His entourage followed him everywhere, laughing at his jokes, basking in his confidence. And Susan was always there—smiling, radiant, untouchable. She existed in a world that seemed just out of Wally's reach.

But he wasn't giving up.

For weeks, he tried everything to catch her eye. He lingered after practice, throwing perfect passes, hoping she'd glance his way as the cheerleaders wrapped up their routines. She never did. Passing her in the hallways was even worse—his mouth would go dry, his brain would blank, and the best he could manage was a mumbled "Hi" before tripping over his own feet.

Kevin, ever the realist, told him to let it go. "She's not gonna fall for a guy just because he can throw a football, pal."

But Wally was hooked.

And he wasn't about to back down that easily.

One afternoon, after weeks of failed attempts, Wally finally worked up the nerve to do more than just wave awkwardly. He spotted her at the edge of the football field, tying her shoes while the cheerleading squad packed up. Gripping a football like a lifeline, he approached, his heart pounding harder with each step.

"Hey, Susan. You, uh—you're really swell out there. The cheers, I mean. You make the whole team look sharper," he stammered, cringing at how ridiculous it sounded.

Susan paused, looking at him for a moment before giving a polite smile. "Thanks, Wally."

Her brief acknowledgment gave him just enough courage to press on. "I, uh, was thinking maybe sometime you'd like to hang out? Catch a flick or something?"

Before she could answer, Johnny appeared out of nowhere, towering over Wally with his signature swagger. "What's this, Masters? You sweet-talking my girl?" Johnny said, his tone playful but laced with a warning. Wally could feel the unspoken challenge in the air. "Don't make me stick you on water bucket duty." He laughed, and within seconds, a few of his friends had gathered around, already laughing along with him.

Wally froze, his heart pounding in his ears. "I wasn't flirting, we were just talking—"

Johnny cut him off with a laugh, clapping him on the shoulder hard enough to send him stumbling. "Relax, I'm just ribbing you. But maybe stick to football, huh?" He winked at Susan, who shook her head in mild disapproval. "What, babe? Masters knows I'm kidding around." He slung an arm around her and steered her off the field, his friends trailing close behind.

As Johnny swaggered away, Wally's chest tightened. It wasn't the first time Johnny had humiliated him in front of Susan, and each time it stung a little deeper. He was nowhere near fixing his reputation—if anything, he was on the verge of becoming the class clown. That night, as Wally lay in bed, replaying the moment over and over, he wracked his brain for ways to win Susan over.

...

A sharp beep pierced through the memory, pulling Wally back into the hospital room. His heart lurched as the past dissolved, replaced by the harsh fluorescent lights and the empty bed in front of him. Mikey's bed.

Wally's breath caught, his pulse hammering in his ears. His eyes fixed on the sterile sheets, and for a terrifying moment, he could almost see it—Mikey's small body cut open, blood and tubes, gloved hands moving with grim precision. The thought sent a cold wave of nausea through him, his chest tightening painfully.

No. He couldn't think about that. He couldn't handle that. His mind, desperate for escape, slid back into a safer memory.

...

four
. . .

IN THE WEEKS THAT FOLLOWED, Wally's attempts to catch her attention continued, each one more forced than the last. But something else was happening—his throws were improving. The coaches began to notice. During one practice, while they had him throwing passes to receivers running drills, something clicked. The feeling of launching the ball across the field to a sprinting receiver was exhilarating. For the first time, Wally felt like he'd found something he was truly good at.

Wally earned the second-string spot behind Johnny, and Johnny didn't take it well. Wally's repeated attempts to talk to Susan had already been fueling Johnny's irritation, but now, with Wally posing a potential threat to his first-string position, Johnny's hostility ramped up. He seemed determined to undermine Wally at every turn, going out of his way to help Jimmy Bates reclaim the second-string spot. Johnny's influence over the team was undeniable, and it wasn't long before the rest of the players followed his lead, showing Wally little respect both on and off the field.

One afternoon after practice, as Wally made his way to the

locker room, Johnny and his friends intercepted him. "You really got a thing for my girl, don't ya, Masters?"

Wally straightened, bracing himself. "I don't see a ring on her finger."

Johnny laughed, but before Wally could react, he was slammed hard against the lockers. "You think you can take what's mine?"

"I didn't realize Susan was your property," Wally shot back, refusing to back down. "Does she know?"

Johnny's eyes flared, and he shouted to his friends, "Lookie here, boys, this joker's got a mouth!" His friends whooped in response. "That big mouth of yours is gonna land you in hot water, Masters."

Wally's first instinct was to fight back—he'd learned how to throw a decent punch. But something held him back. Fighting now, in front of Johnny's friends, wouldn't change anything. Still, Wally longed to wipe that smug smirk off Johnny's face.

He stood firm against the lockers, fists clenched at his sides, as Johnny shoved him again, this time landing a solid hit to his gut. Wally doubled over slightly, pain flaring, but he kept his eyes fixed on the ground, refusing to show any weakness.

"You're pathetic," Johnny sneered, his face inches from Wally's. "Stay away from Susan."

As Johnny strode off, Wally stood there, chest heaving, body burning with anger. He knew he could've fought back, but what would that have solved? Susan liked Johnny, or at least it seemed that way. The last thing Wally wanted was to make things worse with her.

Football season was winding down, and Wally had spent most of it as a safety. In the final few games, the coaches rotated him through different positions, even giving him a shot on special teams, where he pulled off a couple of solid punt returns. Then, everything changed when Johnny sprained his hamstring and was sidelined for the last two games of the season. For a senior like Johnny, the timing couldn't have been worse—missing those critical games might have cost him a shot at being recruited for college ball.

For Wally, this was his moment to shine. He stepped into Johnny's role as quarterback. The experience was nothing short of exhilarating. They lost one game but won the other, and during that victory, Wally threw his first touchdown pass in a varsity game. That moment ignited something inside him —a spark of confidence and a sense of belonging he'd never fully felt before. Even his teammates, who had been fiercely loyal to Johnny Wilds all season—some of whom had taunted Wally in the locker room—applauded his efforts on the field. Their grudging respect felt like a small but hard-earned triumph. As the season came to a close, Wally found himself energized, already counting down the days until next season.

Without football to keep him distracted, the school year seemed to stretch endlessly, each day more grueling than the last. Wally found himself stuck on the sidelines of life, forced to watch as Johnny and Susan's relationship unfolded right in front of him. Every shared laugh, every casual touch between them was like a fresh jab, a reminder of everything Wally wanted but couldn't have.

Johnny was back on his feet before long, but his frustration over missing the end of the football season seemed to bubble over in new, uglier ways. His swagger had turned meaner, his charm giving way to cruelty. He zeroed in on Wally as a target, channeling his irritation into relentless petty aggression. In the hallways, Johnny would shove Wally hard into the lockers, muttering insults just loud enough for him to hear. "Watch where you're going, Masters," he'd sneer, his smirk daring Wally to fight back. Other times, Johnny would tackle him from behind without warning, sending Wally sprawling as laughter echoed from Johnny's friends.

Kevin, ever loyal, would trail behind, his thin, wiry frame

a stark contrast to Johnny's hulking presence. He knew the sting of being a target all too well and could empathize with Wally in a way that others couldn't. Yet, when Johnny and his friends turned their attention toward him, Kevin would instinctively shrink under their gaze, knowing he wasn't the least bit intimidating. His shoulders would hunch as he avoided eye contact, muttering something about needing to get to class.

"He's just a blowhard," Kevin would say, handing Wally a comic or a soda in an attempt to lighten the mood. But his words often felt hollow, a thin veil over the harsh truth they both understood—Johnny wasn't going to stop anytime soon.

At first, Johnny's ambushes left Wally blindsided. The first two tackles came out of nowhere, sending him sprawling to the floor amidst the laughter of onlookers. But by the third time, Wally had learned to stay sharp, keenly aware of his surroundings whenever Johnny was nearby. One day, as Johnny sprinted toward him for another surprise tackle, Wally pretended not to notice. At the last possible second, he dropped low, and as Johnny tumbled over him, Wally surged upward, using Johnny's momentum to flip him through the air. Johnny landed with a loud crash on his back, the sound echoing down the hall. The stunned laughter from nearby students said it all—Johnny wouldn't be trying any more surprise tackles after that.

When the student council began promoting the Spring Formal Dance, Wally scrambled. He didn't want to take anyone else, but going stag wouldn't exactly help his reputation. If he and Kevin showed up without dates, they would be forever branded as grade-A loners. Despite their best efforts, neither Wally nor Kevin managed to secure dates.

They couldn't just skip the dance, so they volunteered to join the band—Kevin naturally on keyboards, thanks to all the piano lessons from his mother, and Wally on tambourine and shakers. It was the perfect excuse to be part of the action without drawing attention to the fact that neither of them had a date. From their spot on the stage, they could watch everything unfold, blending into the background while still feeling like they belonged.

While the other band stand-ins took their turn on stage, Wally and Kevin slipped away for a 15-minute break. Wally stood beside Kevin at the refreshment table, sipping punch while Kevin rambled enthusiastically about a new comic book. Wally nodded absently, but his friend's words quickly faded into the background. His attention kept drifting, his gaze wandering across the room.

His eyes found Susan across the room. She stood with Johnny and her friends, radiant in a pale blue dress that shimmered softly under the lights. The way she moved, the way she laughed—it was effortless, magnetic. Wally's heart sank as he watched her, the sharp weight of reality settling in. He knew he didn't stand a chance, not with Johnny by her side, not in this lifetime. But even knowing that, he couldn't look away. Something about her held him captive, no matter how much it hurt.

That's when Johnny, surrounded by his football buddies, made a cruel joke. "Looks like you're wearing your grandma's curtains, babe," he said, loud enough for everyone nearby to hear. His friends burst into laughter, but when they saw Susan's face flush with embarrassment, the laughter faded.

"You're so mean," Susan muttered, clearly hurt, but Johnny, riding the attention, didn't stop.

"Aw, c'mon, don't be so touchy. It's just a gag!" he shouted, his voice rising above the music.

Wally, standing just a few feet away, saw the hurt in Susan's eyes, and something inside him snapped. It was one thing for Johnny to treat him poorly—but seeing him be so rotten to Susan was another. Before he could think, Wally closed the distance and stepped between them, his voice firm.

"One of these days, everyone's gonna see what a big phony you are."

Johnny's grin vanished as he sized Wally up. "What's your deal, Masters?"

"My deal is you're a loudmouthed creep!" Wally said, his heart pounding but his voice steady.

For a moment, silence hung in the air. Johnny's friends exchanged uneasy glances, sensing the tension shift. Then Johnny, clearly caught off guard, scoffed. "I told you that mouth of yours is gonna get you in hot water!" He scoffed and shoved Wally hard into the refreshments table, knocking over a bowl of punch. The music from the stand-in band stopped abruptly, and a collective gasp rippled through the room. Someone shouted, "Fight!"

Johnny lunged at Wally, grabbing his shirt and landing a solid punch to his nose. Blood poured down Wally's face as he staggered back, trying to regain his balance.

"Stop it, Johnny!" Susan cried, grabbing his arm. He swatted her away—probably harder than he meant to—and sent her tumbling to the floor. Her face flushed with humiliation as she scrambled to her feet, eyes bright with tears. "We're done, Johnny! You and I are through!" she shouted, disappearing into the crowd.

"Susan!" Johnny called after her, panic creeping into his voice. "That was an accident, I didn't mean—" But she was already gone.

He turned back to Wally, a new fury blazing in his eyes—murderous and unhinged. The look sent something snapping inside Wally, pushing him past his breaking point.

Fueled by a surge of anger he couldn't contain, he charged forward, slamming into Johnny and knocking him into the crowd. Chaos erupted as Wally threw a flurry of wild punches, aiming for Johnny's sides, even as Johnny wrestled him to the ground. But Wally wasn't finished. He twisted free with surprising ease, driving a sharp elbow into Johnny's jaw.

There was a strange, unshakable confidence in the way Wally fought—like he had been doing it his whole life. Blow after blow landed with precision, forcing Johnny to stumble back, retreating into the safety of his friends. For the first time, Johnny looked shaken, even afraid, as he cowered behind the very crowd that once cheered him on.

Johnny's eyes darted past Wally, catching sight of a teacher —the chaperone—pushing through the crowd. His expression shifted from fury to irritation. With a groan, he spun around and sprinted for the exit.

"This isn't over, Masters!" he shouted over his shoulder, his voice echoing through the gym.

Just then, the teacher reached Wally, taking in his bloodied face with a sharp intake of breath. "Come with me," he said firmly, gripping Wally by the arm and steering him away.

...

five

. . .

WALLY FELT eyes on him and looked over to where Susan still sat with her parents in the hospital waiting room. Even from here, he could see the tears in her eyes and the worry etched into her face. That expression—fear and misery, now with the added weight of a mother's worry. She was still furious with him, too, but the fear overshadowed everything else.

The harsh fluorescent lights buzzed faintly, and the smell of antiseptic hung heavy in the air. But even with the anger radiating from Susan, all Wally could see was the girl he had found later that night—so hurt and vulnerable. The memory pulled at him, dragging him back.

...

They rushed out of the gym and into the hallways. Wally recognized the teacher as one of the math instructors for the upper grades—likely geometry or advanced algebra.

"What's your name, son?" the teacher asked.

"Wally Masters," Wally replied.

"Did Johnny and his boys jump you?" The teacher's tone suggested he was all too familiar with Johnny Wilds and his crew of bullies.

"They were out of control, sir," Wally said, doing his best to sound respectful.

Just then, Kevin burst through the door, eyes wide. "There you are!"

He hurried over, and Wally felt a wave of relief. Having Kevin by his side was a good thing—Kevin's polite, academic reputation was solid.

"Kevin, this boy your friend?" the teacher asked. Of course, he knew Kevin. He was a math teacher, after all.

"Yes, Mr. Greene," Kevin said, standing straight. "He's my best friend."

"Well, that settles it," Mr. Greene said, nodding. "We'll make sure those boys get suspended for this."

"Thank you, sir," Wally said.

"You'd better get that nose looked at," Mr. Greene instructed. "Go see Miss Holly at the front entrance—she'll patch you up. Not sure she can do much about that bloodstain on your shirt, though."

"Yes, sir," Wally said, and he and Kevin made their way to the front of the gym, where a few ladies sat at a table taking tickets. "I was told to find... Miss Holly?" Wally asked awkwardly, feeling strange about using her first name.

"It's Miss Isaacs," a woman corrected, standing quickly when she saw the blood on Wally's face and shirt. Her short, puffed-up hair bobbed as she moved to him. "Come on, let's get you to the nurse's office," she said, gently guiding him by the elbow.

Miss Isaacs led both boys into the room as Kevin watched her carefully inspect Wally's nose. "That looks broken," she said, placing her thumbs against the bridge of his nose. With a quick movement, she straightened it, and Wally let out a howl of pain. She quickly taped the bridge of his nose and stuffed his nostrils with cotton to stop the bleeding.

"You'll have black eyes for a couple of weeks, but as long as you don't bump it again, you should heal just fine," Miss Isaacs said, stepping back. "Now, unless you've got a spare shirt lying around, you might want to head home and get cleaned up."

"Yes, ma'am. Thank you, Miss Isaacs," Wally and Kevin said in unison before excusing themselves.

"Think the band'll mind?" Wally asked, running a hand over his blood-stained shirt.

"Probably," Kevin said with a chuckle. "I would. You need some rest, pal."

"Aw, quit making such a fuss," Wally said with a dismissive wave. "I can still hang with you fellas on stage." But as he spoke, a wave of dizziness washed over him. Kevin steadied him with a hand on his shoulder, guiding him to a bench in the hallway.

"You're in no shape for that," Kevin said, helping Wally get settled. "Now just sit tight. The band's shorthanded, so I gotta go help. But if you stay put and keep outta trouble, I'll be right back to take you home."

"Alright, alright, fine," Wally sighed. "I'll just sit here a while."

Kevin seemed satisfied enough and rushed off to rejoin the band.

"By myself," Wally added under his breath.

After a few minutes of sitting, the dizziness faded. Feeling restless, he meandered through the dim, empty hallways, his footsteps soft but echoing faintly against the linoleum floors. The contrast between the quiet corridors and the vibrant energy of the gym was stark. The muffled hum of dance music seeped through the walls, mingling with the occasional clink of punch glasses and bursts of laughter.

Eventually, Wally stopped in front of the trophy case, his

eyes drawn to the gold-plated plaques and polished awards within. The soft glow of the display lights reflected off the glass, casting faint patterns on the linoleum floor. He scanned the names and dates, letting his mind wander as he imagined the stories behind each achievement. The quiet around him felt heavy but oddly soothing, offering a brief reprieve from the music, laughter, and his own swirling thoughts.

As his gaze settled on the plaques commemorating past all-state teams, a fleeting daydream surfaced—his own name etched onto one of those plaques someday, a legacy in polished gold. The thought was interrupted by a sound that broke through the stillness—a soft sniffle.

Wally turned, his brow furrowing as he caught a flicker of movement out of the corner of his eye. Behind another trophy case, the faint shimmer of a pale blue dress caught the light.

"Susan?" he called gently, taking a cautious step forward.

He approached slowly, rounding the corner to find her sitting on the floor, her face buried in her hands, shoulders trembling with quiet sobs. For a moment, he hesitated, unsure of what to do. Then, softly, he asked, "You okay?"

She hesitated before lowering her hands, her tearful eyes meeting his for a brief moment before she looked away. "Did Johnny do that to you?"

"I've had worse," Wally said with a small shrug, lowering himself to the floor. He leaned back against the wall, keeping a respectful distance, but close enough to talk quietly.

"I—I didn't think he'd be like that. Not in front of everyone," she whispered, her voice shaking.

"People act different when they're trying to impress their friends," Wally said gently. "You deserve better."

Susan glanced at him, her expression softening. "Thanks, Wally. Really."

"Hey, you'd do the same," Wally said, trying to downplay it, though he couldn't shake the feeling that this moment was different. For the first time, it felt like she actually saw him—

Living A Dream

not as the comic book nerd or the try-hard on the football field, but as someone who genuinely cared.

"Wanna get some air?" Wally asked, nodding toward the exit. To his surprise, Susan nodded, her expression softening as if she welcomed the chance to escape. He quickly stood, offering his hand to help her to her feet, and held the door open as they stepped outside into the crisp March evening.

...

The sharp clang of a metal tray hitting the floor jolted Wally from his thoughts. He glanced toward the hallway, where two nurses hurried to gather the scattered tools. Then, his eyes drifted back to the empty bed. How was the surgery going?

Exhaustion pressed down on Wally like a weight as he sat alone, his hands limp on his knees. He knew Mikey was where he needed to be, that a pediatric surgeon was the right one for the job—but that did nothing to ease the crushing helplessness. He was caught between feeling too heavy to move and a restless urge to climb the walls, to do something —anything—to help.

He let out a long sigh and turned toward the window, his gaze landing on Susan. *His* Susan. It hadn't always been this hard. The early years were a struggle, but they had each other. They made time. And Wally would never forget the night everything changed between them.

The memory took hold, vivid and unrelenting, pulling him back as if he were living it all over again.

...

. . .

The cool night air hit them as they walked into the quiet courtyard. A faint breeze rustled the bare branches of the oak trees that lined the edges of the school grounds, their skeletal forms silhouetted against a night sky dotted with stars. The smell of damp earth and the faint tang of salt from the Chesapeake Bay lingered in the air, mingling with the faint scent of someone's cigarette smoke carried on the wind.

Susan tucked her hands into her jacket, her breath forming faint clouds as she spoke. She began venting about Johnny—how distant he'd been lately, how off she'd been feeling for weeks, and how much it was all starting to weigh on her. Wally didn't say much; he just listened, the cool air sharpening his focus. For once, it was just the two of them, without the noise of the gym or the imposing shadow of Johnny Wilds looming over them. In the quiet of the night, Wally saw her differently—unguarded, vulnerable, and somehow even more real.

As the night wore on, they found a quiet bench beneath the stars, their conversation flowing easily, touching on everything and nothing at all. The world around them seemed to fade away. Wally still felt like the underdog, but for the first time, he didn't feel invisible to her. In the soft glow of the moonlight, Susan looked at him in a way that made him wonder—maybe, just maybe, he had a shot.

By the time they wandered back inside, the dance was winding down. The music had slowed, and the crowd had thinned to a scattering of couples swaying on the floor. Johnny was nowhere to be seen. On stage, Kevin was still with the band, playing a love ballad that filled the gym with a bittersweet melody.

Wally glanced at Susan and took a chance. "Hey, uh, how 'bout a dance?" he asked, trying to sound casual as he flashed his best grin.

Susan hesitated, her eyes searching his face. For a moment, it seemed like she might say yes. Her lips parted slightly, and a small, uncertain smile tugged at the corners of her mouth. But before she could respond, two of her girlfriends rushed over, their voices urgent.

"Susan! Are you okay? I saw what that monster did to you…" Their words trailed off into hushed tones as they guided her away, casting worried glances in her direction.

Wally stood frozen, his hand still half-raised, watching as they led her toward the doors. Just before she disappeared from the room, Susan turned back. Her eyes locked with Wally's, and for a brief moment, the world seemed to hold its breath.

It was undeniable. Something was there—a spark, faint but unmistakable.

…

Wally lifted his head, his eyes drifting to Susan, whose head hung low as her parents sat quietly beside her. She was avoiding his gaze, and the ache in his chest deepened. He couldn't pinpoint what had caused the rift between them, but whatever it was, he felt an overwhelming urge to fix it.

Winning her over had once felt like the greatest triumph of his life. By the time their senior year rolled around, he had been walking on air, caught up in the magic of a relationship that felt untouchable. It had been perfect—or at least, it had seemed that way. Now, sitting in this cold, sterile room, all he wanted was to find a way back to that feeling, to that time when everything between them felt whole.

…

. . .

The summer before their senior year had been different. Wally and Kevin spent those months working at the local drive-in movie theater, rotating between concessions, ticket admissions, and cleanup duty. The job was easy enough—most of the time, they got to goof around, snack on popcorn, and catch glimpses of the movies playing on the big screen while helping customers. It was fun in its own way, but for Wally, the summer felt like it was slipping through his fingers.

At the start of June, Wally finally convinced Susan to go out with him. She had broken up with Johnny during the school dance at the end of junior year and seemed to welcome the distraction.

So when Susan had a free night at the beginning of summer, Wally jumped at the chance. One perk of working at the drive-in was the free admission, a benefit Wally was finally putting to good use. As he pulled his old Chevy into the gravel lot, the familiar crunch of tires on stones blended with the distant hum of cicadas—a soundtrack he'd grown used to over the past few weeks. But tonight, everything felt different. His heart thudded in his chest, nerves fluttering as the reality of his first official date with Susan hit him.

Adjusting the rearview mirror, he stole a quick glance at her. She sat quietly, gazing out the window, her soft blonde hair catching the golden light of the setting sun. The faint glow gave her an almost ethereal quality. She wore a simple red sundress that matched the ribbon tied neatly in her hair, and at that moment, she looked so effortlessly beautiful that Wally had to remind himself to breathe.

Even though he knew the drive-in like the back of his hand, tonight it felt transformed. The rows of parked cars and glowing screen held a kind of magic.

"Do you like drive-ins?" Wally asked, doing his best to sound casual.

Susan smiled, her eyes lighting up. "I've never been to one. But I've always wanted to."

Wally's throat tightened, and all he could manage was a nod as he eased the car into a spot. After a moment, he reached for the bulky speaker, carefully hooking it to the window.

"I think tonight's movie is *The Apartment*. My friend Kevin said it's good."

"I've heard about it," Susan replied. "I love romantic comedies."

Wally exhaled, the tension in his chest easing. Relief swept over him—he was glad he'd picked something she might enjoy. As the opening credits began to roll, Wally couldn't help sneaking glances at her, hoping the evening would leave the right impression. They shared a bag of popcorn, their fingers brushing occasionally in the dim light. Each accidental touch sent a jolt through Wally's stomach, and he noticed Susan didn't pull away. In fact, she began to smile softly each time their hands met—a small gesture that made his heart pound.

Halfway through the movie, the cool evening air met the warm interior of the car, fogging up the windows. Susan giggled, leaning forward to trace a small heart in the condensation on the passenger-side glass.

Wally, mustering a bit of courage, drew a heart on his own fogged-up window. Susan laughed softly, her eyes sparkling as she turned toward him.

"Didn't take you for a softie," she teased, a playful lilt in her voice.

"Hey, I'm not a softie!" Wally shot back, feigning offense, though the grin spreading across his face gave him away. His nerves were finally beginning to melt. "But that doesn't mean I can't be a little romantic."

Susan tilted her head, her smile lingering as she looked at him. "I like romantic," she said quietly.

The movie played on, but neither of them paid it much attention. Their voices rang through the car as they talked, sharing stories about school, favorite songs, and memories from their childhoods. The world beyond the car faded away, and by the time the credits rolled, they were leaning closer, their laughter mingling in the small, intimate space, the connection between them unmistakable.

On the drive home, the warm summer breeze flowed through the open windows, carrying the scent of freshly cut grass and distant honeysuckle. Wally couldn't stop smiling, his heart full as he glanced at Susan. In the dim light, she looked like a dream come true, her soft blonde hair catching the glow of the dashboard.

…

Wally let out a soft chuckle, the memory so vivid that he could have sworn he was actually sitting in his car, looking at Susan. He hadn't even realized his eyes were closed until he opened them.

That was when Susan's eyes finally met his. The faint amusement lingering on his face clashed sharply with the gravity of the situation, and her expression hardened. Their son was in surgery, fighting for his life, and here Wally was—sitting there as if something was funny.

Susan's jaw tightened, her eyes flashing with anger before she turned away abruptly, folding her arms.

The realization hit Wally like a jolt—what was he doing? Why couldn't he stay in the present, focused on how serious things were now? Why did his mind keep dragging him into the past? He couldn't blame Susan for her anger. But as he looked at her, his mind began to slip again—back to the early days of their relationship, back to a time when everything had felt so fresh, so new, and so full of promise.

six
. . .

IT WAS THEIR FIFTH DATE, and summer was nearly over. Wally had been sure they'd get to spend a lot of time together, but between his work schedule and all the summer camps Susan attended, finding a free evening hadn't been easy. Every time they tried to make plans, something seemed to get in the way.

They had just come from the school sock hop—a whirlwind of spinning records, shared laughter, and stolen moments on the dance floor—followed by the sweet simplicity of milkshakes at the diner. Wally still couldn't believe his luck. Susan was the prettiest girl he'd ever seen, and each date only made him like her more.

As they slid into a red vinyl booth under the glow of a neon clock, Wally tried to play it cool. But when his foot accidentally bumped hers under the table, his face flushed crimson.

"Oops! Sorry," he stammered, rubbing the back of his neck.

Susan giggled. "It's fine, Wally. I'm not made of glass, you know."

Her teasing eased his nerves, and he let out a soft chuckle

as the waiter placed a milkshake between them, complete with two straws. They leaned in together, their faces just inches apart, sharing the creamy vanilla treat.

"I still think you've got a future in line dancing if football doesn't work out," Susan said with a playful nudge.

"No way!" Wally shot back, grinning as his confidence grew. "I had two left feet on that dance floor."

Susan smiled and gave a little shrug. "I thought it was cute."

When the milkshake was gone, Wally offered to walk Susan home. The cool night air wrapped around them as they strolled down the quiet street, the soft chirping of crickets filling the silence. When they reached her front porch, Wally hesitated, his hands shoved deep into his pockets as Susan turned to face him under the glow of the porch light.

"I, uh, had a great time," he mumbled, shifting awkwardly from foot to foot, his nerves bubbling to the surface.

"I did too," Susan replied, her eyes sparkling under the porch light. She lingered, her gaze steady, as if waiting for something more.

Wally took a deep breath, feeling his pulse hammering in his chest. This was the moment. "Susan, I—" he began, but before he could finish, his foot slipped off the edge of the porch step. He stumbled, flailing for balance, and barely managed to catch himself in time. Susan gasped, startled, before bursting into laughter, her hand flying to her mouth. Wally straightened up, his face burning crimson, and muttered, "I meant to do that."

His voice was shaky, but the laughter dancing in Susan's eyes eased his embarrassment. She smiled at him, and Wally felt the awkwardness between them melt into something lighter.

"You see, I knew you were a dancer," she teased, stepping closer to him.

Living A Dream

Wally laughed, shaking his head. "Like I said. Two left feet."

"Who needs a right?" Susan said, her voice soft. She reached up, brushing a stray lock of hair from his forehead with a touch so light it sent a shiver down his spine.

Wally's breath caught, his heart hammering in his chest. Before he could overthink it, he leaned in. Susan's eyes fluttered shut just as their lips met—a gentle, sweet kiss that seemed to make the world around them fade away. The soft chirping of crickets, the cool night air, even the glow of the porch light—it all vanished, leaving just the two of them at that moment.

When they pulled apart, Susan smiled, her cheeks flushed and her eyes brighter than ever. "I really like you, Wally Masters."

Wally grinned. "And I really like you, Susan Patterson."

...

A sharp buzzer echoed down the hospital hallway, jolting Wally back to the present once again. The sterile scent of disinfectant hung thick in the air, blending with the low murmur of conversations and the rhythmic squeak of nurses' shoes on polished floors. Wally shifted in his chair, glancing toward Susan. Her eyes were fixed on the ground, avoiding his, her posture tense and closed off. The distance between them felt heavier than the walls of the hospital itself.

Wally leaned back, letting out a slow breath. Fighting the memories was useless—they kept crashing over him, relentless and uninvited. He couldn't do anything for Mikey, or for himself, right now. All he could do was try to get his head straight, to figure himself out so he could be there for Mikey if —and when—his son woke up.

His eyes drifted shut, and the weight of the moment began to blur. His mind slid back to senior year, to dating Susan when everything felt simple and bright. They hit it off right away, and from that point on, they were practically joined at the hip. Kevin was always with them, but no one ever thought of him as a third wheel. Together, they were the three musketeers, each bringing something unique to their little trio.

...

When Susan first saw Kevin's stacks of comics, she gasped, her eyes widening in amazement. "You really have all these?" she asked, picking up a copy of *The Flash* and flipping through it.

Kevin nodded enthusiastically, launching into a detailed explanation of why this particular issue was significant. Susan had never been into comics, but she was a good sport. She humored Kevin, joining in on their reading sessions every now and then. Kevin's passion was infectious, and she enjoyed seeing the spark in his eyes as he explained the intricate storylines and superhero dynamics.

Wally and Kevin would always get excited about new issues coming out, counting down the days until the latest editions hit the shelves. They'd often drag Susan along to the comic book store after school. While she never quite shared their level of enthusiasm, she appreciated their hobby. To pass the time, she would bring her own reading materials—*Seventeen* magazines or one of her beloved Nancy Drew mysteries—curling up on the couch while the boys debated the merits of Batman versus The Flash.

Friday nights remained sacred as movie nights at Kevin's house, but now Susan was part of the ritual. Kevin's family welcomed her warmly, treating her like one of their own. His mother always made extra popcorn, and his older sister enjoyed striking up conversations with Susan.

Kevin's father, a doctor with a passion for history, would occasionally join them, offering mini-lessons on the historical accuracy—or lack thereof—of whatever movie they were watching. Whenever a scene involved injuries or medical treatments, he couldn't resist commenting on the practices of the time, explaining what real doctors would do differently. Kevin soaked it all in, fascinated, and Wally—though he'd never admit it—found himself listening closely too.

Even though Wally and Kevin no longer worked at the Drive-In theater due to their busy school schedules, they couldn't resist the allure of the outdoor screen. Every few weeks, they'd load up Kevin's Ford Falcon with snacks, park in the lot, and catch the latest flick. Wally and Susan would sit together in the front seat, and Kevin would sprawl across the back, munching on a bag of popcorn and providing running commentary that ranged from hilarious to annoyingly insightful.

As football season kicked into gear, their schedules became even busier. Wally threw himself into practices, determined to make the most of his starting position as quarterback. Susan, now a seasoned cheerleader, led routines with effortless grace. Kevin, though not athletic, was always there to support his friends. Every Friday night, he perched in the bleachers with a notebook in hand, diligently keeping statistics on all the players.

After each game, Kevin would eagerly share his findings, rattling off numbers and percentages with the precision of a seasoned analyst. "You threw for 225 yards, completed 16 of 22 passes, and had two touchdown throws tonight," he'd say, his voice brimming with pride.

"You're such a nerd, Kev!" Wally would tease, giving him a playful shove. But Kevin was undeterred. If anything, he only leaned in more—launching into excited explanations about muscle memory, reaction time, and how different injuries could impact a quarterback's throwing arm. His fascination with anatomy and medicine was infectious. He'd talk about how tendons and ligaments worked, or why ice baths helped with recovery, slipping in terms like *"rotator cuff"* and *"lactic acid"* as easily as most guys talked about last night's game.

Wally would roll his eyes, but secretly, he loved the updates—especially as his stats started to look more impressive with each passing game. There was something reassuring about Kevin's confidence, about the way he seemed to understand how the body worked and how to keep it from falling apart.

Between school, football, and cheerleading, their days were packed, but they always carved out time for each other. After practice, they'd pile into Kevin's car and set off for their next adventure—bowling, catching the latest movie, or just hanging out in Kevin's living room with a stack of comics and books. Susan introduced them to sock hops at the school gym, and the boys quickly got hooked, surprised to find they weren't half-bad on the dance floor.

Even the simple moments—like sharing fries at the local diner or goofing around at the arcade—felt like grand adventures. They laughed until their sides hurt, danced until their feet were sore, and talked about everything and nothing at all.

Any free evening was spent together, a trio bound by friendship and the simple joys of being young—until Kevin would shoot them a knowing look and declare he was tired and ready to turn in a little early. Then Wally and Susan would have some time alone, enjoying the quiet thrill of getting to know each other better.

. . .

...

As Wally reflected back on the end of that football season, the year he had started as quarterback, the memories felt fragmented, as if someone had torn whole chapters from his story. Two conflicting narratives swirled in his head, tangled and unclear. He struggled to make sense of what had happened, the haze of time blurring the edges of the season and the events that followed. The more he tried to grasp it, the more elusive it seemed.

...

The roar of the crowd thundered in Wally's ears as he jogged onto the field, the adrenaline coursing through him like electricity. This was it—the state championship. The floodlights above bathed the field in a bright, almost theatrical glow, turning the crisp night into a stage set for triumph. Every eye in the packed stands seemed fixed on him, the weight of expectation pressing against his chest. Wally's heart pounded. College scouts were watching. His future, everything he'd worked for, hinged on this game.

The first quarter started strong. Wally stayed focused, hitting a few key passes that pushed his team down the field. Their running back spotted an opening and broke through the defense, sprinting into the endzone for their first touchdown. The crowd erupted, the cheers echoing like music in Wally's ears. Their next drive ended with a clean field goal, putting them ahead 10-3 as the quarter came to a close.

By the second quarter, Wally was in his element. He connected passes with pinpoint precision, dodged tackles with effortless agility, and read the defense like a seasoned veteran. His confidence ignited the team, and they rallied around him, matching his energy and determination. Drive after drive, they widened the gap, leaving their opponents scrambling. By halftime, Wally had the stadium in the palm of his hand. Scouts in the stands couldn't look away—this wasn't just a good game; it was the kind of performance that changed futures. Every throw, every play was another step closer to the scholarships he had only dared to dream about. His future no longer felt distant or abstract; it was right there, almost tangible, shimmering within reach.

In the third quarter, Wally pulled off the kind of play that athletes relive for years. Faking a pass, he pivoted sharply and felt something pull in his ankle, but he pushed through, sprinting straight up the middle of the field. He dodged defenders left and right, tearing up 40 yards in a single breathtaking run.

The crowd exploded, chanting his name—then fell silent as they watched Wally limp to the sidelines. The second-string quarterback took over while the trainer knelt beside Wally, examining his ankle with a frown. After some massaging, the trainer taped it tightly and cleared him to go back in.

When Wally returned to the field and rejoined the huddle, the crowd erupted all over again. He wasn't about to let a minor injury keep him from playing the game of his life. For Wally, it was the thrill of being exactly where he was meant to be. His future stretched out before him—college, maybe even the NFL—everything he'd worked for falling perfectly into place.

When the final whistle blew, his team stood victorious. Wally was swarmed by teammates, fans, and coaches, the cheers and pats on the back overwhelming. As he scanned the field, his eyes searched for the one person who mattered most. Susan. He found her near the bleachers, but something was wrong. Despite her bright red cheerleader outfit, she wasn't cheering like the others. Instead, she stood fidgeting, her face pale, her hands twisting nervously. She looked anxious—almost on the verge of tears. And not happy tears.

Confused, Wally ran to her, his excitement still pulsing through him. He swept her up in his arms, spinning her around, hoping to bring some joy to the moment. Susan forced a smile, but it didn't reach her eyes. Her expression didn't match the celebration surrounding them, and for the first time that night, Wally's confidence faltered. He couldn't understand why she wasn't sharing in his victory, and the uneasy feeling that settled in his chest dulled the thrill of the win. Something was wrong.

"What's going on, Suze? I thought you'd be happy for me. This is for *us!*" Wally said, his excitement tinged with irritation as he struggled to understand her reservation.

"I am... I *am* happy," Susan replied, forcing another weak smile. But her voice wavered, and her eyes flickered with something she wasn't saying. "At least I'm trying..." Her words trailed off, barely audible.

Wally opened his mouth to press her, but before he could, a swarm of teammates surrounded him, cheering and hoisting him onto their shoulders. "Wally! Wally!" they chanted, carrying him off the field as the crowd roared. He tried to reach for Susan, his arm outstretched, but the distance between them grew too quickly. All he could do was watch as she lowered her head, wiped a tear from her cheek, and turned away, slipping off the field before he could stop her.

The locker room was a blur of applause and celebration. His teammates shouted victory chants, slapping him on the back and calling him the star of the night. Wally forced a smile, accepting their congratulations, but his mind wasn't in the room. He couldn't stop thinking about Susan—about the sadness in her eyes and the way she had disappeared. The thrill of the win felt hollow without her there.

When the chaos died down for a moment and the focus shifted off him, Wally quietly slipped out of the locker room.

He scoured the field, the stands, and the parking lot, calling her name into the night. "Susan?" His voice grew louder, more desperate. "*Susan!*"

Finally, he spotted her. She was sitting behind the steering wheel of her Volkswagen Bug, her head bowed. Wally sprinted toward the car, his breath hitching as he opened the door. "Susan! I've been looking all over for you. What's going on?"

She shook her head, tears streaming freely down her face now. "You go ahead and celebrate. I don't want to ruin it for you…"

"I *can't* celebrate knowing you're like this," Wally said, dropping to his knees so he could meet her eye to eye. "Please. I need to know what's wrong."

For a long moment, Susan just sat there, her hands gripping the steering wheel as if she were trying to steady herself. Finally, she turned to him, her voice trembling as she said, "I'm… I'm pregnant."

The words hung heavy in the air between them, echoing in Wally's ears as if the world had suddenly gone silent. His breath hitched, and he felt the blood rush to his head, leaving him dizzy. He stood abruptly, scanning his surroundings, half wondering if someone might be listening, though the empty parking lot only deepened the isolation of the moment. His gaze drifted upward to the night sky, his mind racing through the plans and promises he'd built for his future. Pregnant? The word hit him like a freight train. He hadn't planned for this—not now, not when everything was finally falling into place.

For a moment, he just stared at Susan, his chest tightening with panic.

"Well? Aren't you going to say something?" she demanded, her voice sharp with frustration, her tear-streaked face searching his for any sign of reassurance.

Wally's eyes met hers, and he struggled to form a coherent thought. "Are... are you sure?" he asked, his voice trembling.

Susan's expression hardened, her patience fraying. "Of course I'm sure!" she snapped. "I knew you'd freak out. I shouldn't have told you."

"No, I'm glad you did," Wally said quickly, though his voice faltered. "I... I just—" He trailed off, his words failing him completely. His eyes dropped as if saying it aloud might make it more real. "You're pregnant."

Susan crossed her arms, her face crumpling as fresh tears welled in her eyes. "I knew this would happen," she sobbed, her voice breaking. "You don't know what to say, and I'm stuck here dealing with this alone."

Wally's initial shock began to give way as he watched her cry, the sight piercing through his own fear. Without thinking, he crouched down in front of her, gently taking her hands in his. He squeezed them tight, grounding himself in the moment, feeling the weight of their reality settle on his shoulders. It was terrifying, but as the panic faded, something stronger began to take its place. He loved her—he'd always known that. And though this was happening far sooner than he'd ever imagined, he knew he wanted a life with her. A family.

"Susan," he said softly, his voice steady now. "I'm not going anywhere. We'll... we'll figure this out."

She nodded, but the uncertainty in her eyes lingered.

"I promise," he said firmly, holding her gaze. "We're in this together."

For the first time that night, a glimmer of hope flickered in her expression. It wasn't much, but it was a start.

For the next week, Wally woke each morning in fear, the weight of his new reality pressing down on him like an immovable force. The thought of bringing a life into the world filled him with a terror that gnawed at his every waking moment. A father. He was going to be a father. The word felt foreign and heavy, a mantle he didn't feel worthy to carry. Was he ready? The answer, at least in his mind, was a resounding no. He was still a kid himself—barely able to manage his own life, let alone guide and provide for another.

Every thought brought more questions than answers. How could he raise a child when he hadn't even figured out who he was? What kind of father would he be? Would he end up being like his own father?

The thought made Wally's chest tighten with panic. Thinking about how much his father had influenced who he was—and the idea of trying to be a father himself—terrified him.

But no matter how deep his fear ran, Wally kept it buried beneath a mask of determination. Susan was always on the verge of tears, her eyes reflecting her own fears and uncertainty. He couldn't add his worries to hers; he had to be strong for both of them. Each day, he held her close and whispered reassurances he wasn't sure he believed himself. "We'll figure this out," he said again and again, as much for his benefit as hers. "I won't let you down."

No matter how scared he was, one thing was certain—he couldn't abandon her. They had nine months to piece together a game plan, and Wally resolved to make every day count.

In the weeks that followed, his life became a whirlwind of decisions and possibilities. His phone buzzed constantly with calls from college coaches and recruiters. Scholarship offers poured in—Notre Dame, Michigan, USC. Each letter and phone call felt like a lifeline, a promise of hope in the midst of his uncertainty. For hours, he sat in the coach's office, poring over brochures and weighing his options. He plotted routes to success, envisioning a future where he could be the provider Susan and the baby deserved.

The thrill of opportunity surged through him, momentarily pushing back the fear. He imagined himself thriving on a college campus, balancing academics and football, and securing a future that could sustain them all.

"I'll make this work, Susan," he said one night, his voice steady despite the weight of his words. "I'll go to college, get my degree, and we'll be set. I'll take care of you and the baby. I promise."

Susan looked up at him, her eyes glistening with tears that blurred the lines between fear and relief. "I should've known you'd stick with me," she said softly. "You'll go to college, and we'll be at every game, cheering you on. You're going to be an amazing football player." Her voice wavered, but her determination was steady. "And maybe I can get a job while you're in school. Just like you said—we're in this together."

They spent hours talking that night, sketching out plans that felt both daunting and hopeful. Wally's resolve hardened with every word. He would accept one of the scholarships, dive into college, and push harder than he ever had before. His dreams weren't just his own anymore—they were for his family.

After dropping Susan off and returning home, Wally lay on his bed, staring up at the cracks in the ceiling. His mind churned with a storm of emotions: fear, hope, determination. His future wasn't the clear-cut path it had seemed a few weeks ago, but it was still his.

It wouldn't be easy. The challenges ahead felt overwhelming, but for the first time, Wally realized he wasn't walking this road alone. He had Susan by his side, their hands clasped tightly as they faced an uncertain future together. He wasn't just fighting for himself anymore—he was fighting for something bigger, something worth every ounce of strength he had.

...

· · ·

Back in the hospital room, Wally sat in silence. He could still remember winning that championship game and receiving a scholarship to the University of Michigan. The memory was so vivid—he could feel the bite of the crisp autumn air, hear the roar of the crowd, and smell the hot dogs and stadium fries drifting across the parking lot. He could even see Susan's face, hear her voice trembling as she told him she was pregnant. It was a moment etched into his mind, clear as day.

But then there was another memory—a conflicting account that gnawed at him like a splinter he couldn't pull free. It contradicted everything, casting doubt on what he thought he knew. He closed his eyes, trying to sort through the haze, to find the edges of the truth, struggling to untangle the web of his memories. Each one felt vivid, real, and undeniable—but they couldn't both be true.

Which version of the past was real? And why did both feel so tangible, so certain? His head throbbed as he tried to piece it all together, the pressure building until he thought he might break.

And then, before he could stop it, that other memory pulled him in.

...

seven

. . .

THE FIRST HALF of the state championship football game was the same in this other memory. Wally was playing the game of his life, every throw crisp and precise, every play executed flawlessly. Scouts in the stands scribbled notes, their eyes fixed on him. Pass after pass, Wally knew he was making an impression. This was his moment.

Then the third quarter came, and everything changed. Wally made a break for it, faking a pass before sprinting down the middle of the field. The gap in the defense was wide, and for a brief, exhilarating moment, he felt unstoppable. But then the strong safety from the opposing team barreled toward him, his shoulder slamming into Wally's knee from the wrong angle. The collision was brutal. Wally felt a searing, white-hot pain shoot through his leg before he hit the ground. His knee twisted unnaturally, and the agony spread like wildfire through his body.

The roar of the crowd abruptly faded into a dull hum, the floodlights above him blurring as his vision swam. He tried to stand, but his leg buckled beneath him, the pain too overwhelming. He collapsed back onto the turf, clutching at his knee as teammates and coaches rushed to his side.

The medical staff swarmed the field, moving quickly to stabilize him. Wally barely registered their voices as they strapped him to a gurney and carted him off. The rest of the night blurred together—the sharp ache in his leg, the concerned faces of friends and teammates, and the doctors briefing him on what little they knew so far.

After hours of uncertainty and a knee surgery, a doctor finally entered the hospital room where Wally lay, his body heavy with pain meds. Wally managed to sit up slightly, his mind foggy but alert enough to catch the doctor's words.

"The good news is, you'll recover and be able to walk again without too much pain," the doctor said, his voice steady but cautious. He hesitated for a moment before delivering the blow. "The bad news? I'm afraid your football days are over, son."

Wally froze, staring into space as the words sank in. He wasn't sure he'd heard correctly, wasn't sure he could even process what had just been said. Football had been everything—his dream, his future, his way out. And now, in a matter of seconds, it was gone. The doctor gave him a brief pat on the shoulder before leaving, but Wally barely noticed.

Wally lay in his hospital bed, staring blankly at the ceiling. His knee throbbed beneath the bandages, but the dull, constant ache was nothing compared to the crushing despair that weighed on him. His dreams—his future—were gone, torn away in an instant. With them went his sense of purpose, leaving a void he didn't know how to fill.

The next few weeks blurred together in a fog of hospital rooms, surgeries, and grueling physical therapy sessions that felt more like punishment than progress. Every strained movement was a cruel reminder of what he had lost. The once-promising scholarship offers vanished as quickly as they had come. The coaches who had once sung his praises now spoke in muted tones, their words careful, their eyes filled with pity that cut deeper than any tackle ever had.

Kevin visited often, balancing his time between Wally's bedside and school, applying for colleges. He'd sit in the chair by the bed, trying to keep the mood light with stories about the latest *Fantastic Four* issue or the most recent episode of their favorite medical drama, *Dr. Kildare*. But even Kevin's easy smile couldn't mask the growing distance between them. Wally could feel it—the unspoken divide. Kevin's future remained untouched, bright, and limitless, while his own felt hollow, a black hole swallowing everything he'd worked for.

Susan visited too, her presence quieter but no less heavy. She sat beside him, her hands resting gently on his, her face etched with worry. She always looked like she had something she wanted to say, something pressing, but the words never came. Wally couldn't meet her eyes. He couldn't bear to see her sadness or her pity. She didn't deserve this—didn't deserve *him*. He was a shadow of the person he'd been, broken and bitter, and he hated himself for it. Part of him wished she would just walk away, save herself from being tied to someone whose life had unraveled so completely.

One night, as the sterile glow of the hospital lights dimmed and the hallway fell silent, Susan leaned over Wally, her eyes full of pleading desperation.

"You'll get through this, Wally," she whispered, her voice trembling, on the verge of breaking. "*We'll* get through it together."

Wally shook his head, a bitter laugh escaping him. His voice was hoarse, heavy with defeat. "Together? You don't want me dragging you down. My future's gone, Susan."

"Wally—" she started, but he cut her off.

"Just go to college without me," he muttered, his eyes fixed on the blank hospital wall. "Kevin's going, and you should too. Don't let me hold you back. Don't ruin your life because of me."

Silence filled the space between them. He could feel her

eyes on him, searching, but he refused to look at her. He didn't want to see the pity or sadness he knew was there.

Then, in a soft, trembling voice, she said, "I can't."

Wally's heart skipped a beat, and for the first time in days, he turned to face her. Her expression was unreadable, but her voice was clear. "What do you mean, you *can't?*"

Tears welled in Susan's eyes, her fingers tightening around his hand. She looked so fragile, her voice barely above a whisper as she finally said, "I'm... I'm pregnant, Wally."

Her words hit him like a tidal wave, crashing over him, leaving him breathless. He stared at her, his mind reeling, the sterile room seeming to tilt and spin. Pregnant? The weight of the revelation pressed down on him, suffocating and inescapable. How could this be happening now—when his whole world was already falling apart?

Wally closed his eyes, the weight of Susan's words crushing him like a tidal wave. He tried to process what she had just said, but the enormity of it was suffocating. His mind raced, each vision of the future he had imagined for them slipping further and further out of reach. He wasn't just losing his dream of playing football—he was losing everything.

The days that followed felt like an endless blur. Wally wrestled with the reality of his future—college was slipping away, and now, he had a baby on the way. It was too much to take in. The weight of it pressed down on him, relentless and inescapable.

Meanwhile, Kevin was preparing for his future, already filling out college applications. His top pick was the University of Michigan. Even before the acceptance letters arrived, Wally could see the spark in his best friend's eyes—Kevin was destined to be a doctor, just like his father. Wally was proud of him, truly, but it only made his own path feel smaller, more suffocating. Kevin was moving forward, full speed ahead,

Living A Dream

while Wally felt stuck, his once-clear future reduced to a foggy uncertainty.

After a week in the hospital, on the night before his discharge, Kevin sat at Wally's bedside, a stack of comics resting in his lap. The silence between them felt heavier than it used to. Kevin flipped idly through the pages, trying to act normal, but Wally knew they were both avoiding the obvious: everything had changed, and neither of them knew how to fix it.

"You're gonna have it all one day, Kev," Wally said quietly, his voice barely above a whisper.

Kevin looked up, frowning. "That was supposed to be you," he said. "You were the one who was going to play football, get the scholarship—everything."

Wally forced a bitter smile, one that didn't quite reach his eyes. "Yeah, well. Life had other plans."

Kevin held his gaze for a long moment, then shook his head. "You've got the whole rest of the school year to figure it out, Wally. I know you will."

Wally didn't answer. He wasn't sure he believed it. But when he looked across the room at Susan, something in him softened. *At least I still have her.*

Throughout his entire hospital stay, Susan never left his side. She held his hand when he was quiet, whispered reassurances when he needed them, and ignored every attempt he made to push her away. At first, he felt embarrassed—ashamed that she was stuck with him, that he had nothing to offer her anymore. But then, something shifted. He saw the way she looked at him, not with pity, but with love. He'd spent so long believing he needed football to be worthy of someone like her, but she had never cared about any of that. She just wanted *him.*

And with her by his side, Wally started to look ahead. His old dreams were gone, but maybe… he could find new ones. He would take care of her, take care of their baby, and build a life for them. She deserved that. And even though the thrill of the game would slowly fade, there was still something—something real, something steady—waiting for him in the future. The thought of spending his life with Susan? That still made his heart race.

When he was discharged, life slowly settled back into something resembling normal. Friday movie nights with Kevin, late-night study sessions, even an occasional sock hop, with Wally hobbling around on his crutches, trying not to aggravate his knee.

After one of their usual movie nights, Wally drove Susan home. The radio hummed softly in the background, neither of them speaking at first. He had so much he wanted to say, but he needed to find the right words. Finally, he pulled the car over to the side of the road, shifting so he could look her in the eyes.

"Hey, Suze," he started, his voice steady but soft. "I know you're worried about what's coming. About everything changing. All the new responsibilities." He took a breath. "I just want you to know—I'm going to make this right. I'll do whatever it takes to take care of you both and give you the life you deserve."

Susan's eyes welled up with tears. She leaned in and kissed his cheek, then rested her forehead against his. "You don't know how much it means to hear you say that."

Wally reached for her hand and gave it a firm, reassuring squeeze. "And even though things didn't turn out the way I thought they would," he said, his lips curling into a small smile, "I'm still excited. To be with you."

Susan smiled through her tears. "Me too."

...

. . .

Living A Dream

Wally lay back in the stiff hospital chair, staring blankly at the ceiling tiles above him. Each square looked identical to the last, forming a monotonous grid that only made his head throb more. He struggled to untangle the web of his memories. Each one felt vivid, real, and undeniable—but they couldn't both be true.

Who had he been? At least he knew that Susan and Mikey were real. But how had he gotten here—to this place in his life?

He was waiting—waiting for news, waiting for the doctor to emerge with some word, any word, about Mikey's surgery. Time stretched endlessly, feeling almost like a dream as Wally stared at the ceiling, images, and memories warring inside his head.

Knowing there was nothing else he could do, Wally forced himself to move—if only to keep from unraveling completely. "I'll head to the cafeteria," he muttered to himself.

As he passed by the waiting room, he noticed that Kevin had returned. Susan's parents sat beside her, their eyes fixed firmly elsewhere, avoiding any eye contact with Wally. His steps faltered, and he hesitated, casting a glance at Susan.

"I'm going to grab something to eat," he said softly, his voice breaking the fragile silence between them. "Do you want me to bring you anything?"

Susan looked up from where she sat. She didn't speak, just shook her head with a small, almost absent motion. Her eyes lingered on him for a moment, her expression unreadable but curious, as though she were trying to decipher something about him. Then she turned away again, retreating back into her own grief.

"Want me to join you, pal?" Kevin asked, getting to his feet.

"Not yet," Wally said, his eyes still on Susan as he gave a subtle shake of his head. "I just need a little more time."

Kevin nodded and sat back down.

Wally swallowed the knot in his throat and continued toward the stairwell, descending quickly as though trying to outrun the weight in his chest. The cafeteria was bright and loud, a jarring contrast to the hushed tension of the waiting room. He bought a sandwich and a soda, more out of routine than hunger, and found a small table in the corner where he could sit alone.

Placing the sandwich on the table, he unwrapped it slowly, his movements mechanical. He took a small bite, chewing without tasting, before putting it back down. The soda remained unopened. He stared at the untouched food in front of him, his appetite gone as quickly as it had come.

The truth was, no amount of food could fill the emptiness clawing at his insides. The weight of the unknown—the surgery, Mikey's fragile condition, the brokenness in Susan's eyes—pressed down on him, making the simple act of eating feel impossible. For a moment, Wally dropped his head into his hands and exhaled deeply, trying to steady himself. But no matter how hard he tried, he couldn't shake the image of Mikey's pale face or the memory of Susan's distant gaze.

The cafeteria buzzed around him—strangers talking, a small group of nurses seated nearby, laughing as if the world hadn't just come to a screeching halt. Wally envied them—their normalcy, their blissful unawareness of how fragile everything really was. But for him, life had cracked wide open, and he wasn't sure it could ever be pieced back together again.

He thought back to his marriage, to the day Mikey was born—a day that should have been crystal clear in his mind. But instead, two conflicting narratives surged forward, colliding like opposing waves. Each memory felt vivid, undeniable, yet impossibly different. He couldn't understand it. How could he have two completely separate versions of the same events? Which ones were real? Which ones belonged to him?

Living A Dream

The confusion gnawed at him, but he pushed the doubt aside and let his thoughts drift, focusing on the first memory. Maybe if he allowed one version to take hold—watched it carefully—he might find a clue about whether it was the real one or not.

...

After the State Championship game, the following months passed in a whirlwind. Wally threw himself into training with an intensity he'd never tapped into before, his every move fueled by a sense of urgency. He was no longer just preparing for the next big game—he was preparing for the future, a future that now held responsibilities far greater than his own dreams.

The pull he'd felt in his ankle during the game turned out to be a strained ligament. So he spent time rehabbing every day until it was back to full functionality, following every exercise and stretch religiously. He found it fascinating how the human body was put together—the intricate network of muscles, tendons, and bones—and was amazed at its ability to heal itself. Kevin's endless enthusiasm for anatomy had started to rub off on him, and Wally couldn't help but get caught up in it a little.

With his ankle strengthening, Wally pushed harder in the weight room, shaved seconds off his sprints, and stayed late after practice, perfecting his throws. He needed to be ready—not just for himself but for the family he was building.

The day their baby was born was unlike anything Wally had ever experienced. He stood in the hospital room, cradling his newborn son, Mikey, in his arms, and the world seemed to fall away. The weight of responsibility melted into an overwhelming sense of purpose, stronger than any touchdown or victory he'd ever known. In that tiny, fragile life, he saw everything he was fighting for. He was both overwhelmed and immeasurably excited by the prospect of being a father.

Orientation at the University of Michigan arrived in a blur of activity. The campus buzzed with excitement, a sea of students eager to dive into their new lives. For Wally, it wasn't quite the college experience he had once imagined. Instead of late-night dorm antics and roommate escapades, he had Susan and their baby to consider. His small off-campus apartment wasn't filled with posters and secondhand couches; it was organized with careful practicality—crib in one corner, textbooks stacked neatly on the kitchen table, and baby supplies tucked into every available space.

Wally had a family to come home to now, and it changed everything. He wasn't living for himself anymore. Every decision he made, every grueling hour on the practice field, every late night in the library, was for them. He carried the image of their future in his mind like a treasured photograph: Susan in the stands, cheering him on as he sprinted down the field; their child clapping wildly, his face glowing with pride. He pictured the day he'd walk across the stage at graduation—diploma in one hand, waving to Susan and his son sitting in the stands with the other, his smile brighter than the sun.

But none of it came without sacrifice. College life moved on around him, full of parties, friendships, and freedom, but Wally's world was different. Late-night hangouts became rare, replaced by diaper changes and bedtime stories. Invitations to parties were easy to decline when he thought about what waited for him at home. His teammates joked about him being the "old man" of the group, but Wally didn't mind.

There were nights, though, when the exhaustion felt insurmountable. After a long day of classes, practice, and part-time work, Wally would collapse into bed, his body aching and his mind racing. Sometimes, the weight of it all pressed so hard he wondered how he'd keep going. But then he'd hear Mikey's soft cry or see Susan's tired smile and the answer would come as clear as a sunrise. He wasn't doing this just for himself.

Every sacrifice, every sleepless night, every ounce of energy—it was all for this. For them. And in that moment, holding his son, Wally knew it was worth it.

One evening, a few weeks after Mikey's birth, Wally sat with a small group of teammates on the dorm steps. The campus was quiet, the air crisp with the scent of autumn leaves. They swapped stories, laughing about grueling practices and impossible professors. One of the players, a lanky receiver named Tyler, shook his head and let out a low whistle.

"I don't know how you do it, pal," Tyler said, his voice filled with genuine admiration. "Like it isn't hard enough worrying about exams and practice. You're juggling school, football, and a brand-new family. You're making the rest of us look bad."

Wally chuckled softly, a quiet pride settling in his chest. "I don't know how I do it either," he admitted. "But every time I look into my little boy's eyes, I find the motivation to work harder and faster. I don't have the option to give up—not when I have them depending on me."

The group fell quiet for a moment, the weight of Wally's words settling over them. One of the linemen nudged him playfully. "Well, if anyone can pull it off, it's you, Masters. You've got that stubborn streak."

Wally laughed, but his gaze drifted upward to the stars. Stubborn streak or not, he knew the road ahead wouldn't be easy. But he also knew one thing for certain—he wouldn't trade it for anything.

Years later, when Wally walked across the stage to receive his diploma, he spotted Susan and their son in the crowd. He raised his hand to them, a promise fulfilled. It wasn't the life he had originally imagined, but it was rich and full, and he was exactly where he was meant to be.

While football had been the perfect springboard for Wally's scholastic career, he no longer envisioned himself pursuing the professional leagues. By the time his senior year rolled around, he knew his time on the field was nearing its end. His old ankle injury had returned, worse this time, eventually requiring surgery. The long weeks of recovery and endless appointments with orthopedic specialists had given him a lot of time to think—and, surprisingly, had sparked something new.

Football had given him discipline, teamwork, and the means to achieve his education, but his ambitions had shifted. What started as a casual curiosity about how the body healed had blossomed into a deeper passion: medicine. His fascination with anatomy, combined with all those hours spent rehabbing his ankle, had opened his eyes to a different kind of purpose. Now, he envisioned a future not in stadiums but in operating rooms.

Susan supported Wally's decision wholeheartedly, especially after witnessing the physical toll football had taken on him. She'd seen him limp home after games, covered in bruises, his body battered but his resolve unshaken. Still, there was a harsh reality to face: Wally's football scholarship would end with his undergraduate degree, and it wouldn't cover the daunting costs of medical school.

Late at night, when the house was quiet and their son was fast asleep, Wally and Susan sat at the kitchen table, poring over finances and scribbling out plans on scraps of paper. They talked through every option, dissecting each one until they both reached the same conclusion—Wally's dream was within reach.

With a mix of scholarships and help from his parents, he enrolled in medical school.

· · ·

...

A child's sharp cry pierced the air at the far end of the cafeteria, yanking Wally back to the present. For a fleeting moment, he wanted to sink back into that memory—to linger in the happiness of when Mikey was born, to relive those early days when he and Susan had been building a life together. He wondered why couldn't they find their way back to the days when they'd laughed together when their small family had been their world.

His thoughts drifted to Susan, still upstairs in the waiting room. She had loved being a mother, had loved raising Mikey. He could still see her face when she first saw him holding Mikey—the awe in her eyes, the soft smile that had said everything words couldn't.

eight

...

BUT THIS TIME, when he thought of Susan giving birth, a different version forced its way forward—uninvited and insistent—muddling his sense of reality. It was the same day, the same moment—but somehow, it wasn't. The details didn't align. The feelings were similar, but not exactly the same.

...

With his career-ending leg injury, Wally had spent months in grueling physical rehabilitation, relearning how to walk and adjust to his new reality. Through it all, Susan stayed by his side, even as her pregnancy progressed into the second trimester.

Despite her growing baby bump, she still loved going out whenever she could. Sock hops became trickier as the months passed, but they still managed to attend one every now and then. More often, though, they found themselves drawn to quieter moments—evening walks along the Chesapeake Bay, where the waves lapped gently against the shore, or picnics in

Living A Dream

open fields, where they could stretch out on a blanket, stare at the clouds, and dream about their future.

Music became another shared escape. Wally and Susan convinced Kevin to start frequenting Sam Goody, the local record store with them, building up a small but cherished vinyl collection. Afterward, they'd head to Kevin's house, dropping the needle on a new record while Kevin sat cross-legged on the floor, poring over the liner notes, rattling off the names of musicians and producers like they were old friends.

And though sock hops were less frequent, Wally and Susan still danced—just the two of them, swaying in Kevin's living room as the music played, wrapped up in each other, lost in a world of their own.

When the school year ended, they had both crossed the stage, high school diplomas in hand. Now in her third trimester with an August due date, Susan did her best to hide her baby bump beneath her gown, trying not to waddle as she accepted her diploma. Wally snickered, teasing her for trying so hard to walk normally, and she swatted his arm with a playful glare.

Kevin had been accepted to the University of Michigan, just as he'd hoped, and would be leaving right around the time Susan and Wally's baby was due. They had one last summer together before everything changed.

Over the past few months, Wally had already started working Saturday shifts at the docks. With school out, he immediately switched to full-time. The paychecks were steady, and the work was honest—but it was exhausting. He came home bone-tired, muscles aching, but the moment he saw Susan, his energy came rushing back. They'd grab Kevin and spend their evenings as they always had, determined to make the most of their last summer together.

By the end of summer, Wally had settled into the rhythm of the job, finding his place among the men on the docks. Everyone knew he was on-call to leave at a moment's notice.

When the call finally came, it was his friend and co-worker, James, who shouted across the docks, "Wally, let's go! Your kid's about to make an entrance!"

When his son, Mikey, was born, Wally felt an overwhelming rush of joy and purpose as he cradled his newborn in his arms. He wished he didn't have to go back to work so soon. They had only given him two days off plus the weekend—just four days to soak in this new chapter of his life before returning to the grind.

In the years that followed, Wally rushed home every evening, eager to celebrate the little milestones. Mikey's first steps. His first words. His first time spitting out strained spinach—Wally didn't blame him; the stuff smelled awful.

But over time, the excitement faded. The days blurred into a routine. Each morning, before the sun rose, Wally hauled himself out of bed, headed to the docks, and worked until his muscles ached. At home, Susan—exhausted from the endless demands of motherhood—always had a list waiting for him. Things that needed fixing. Errands that needed running. Life had settled into a rhythm of obligation, and Wally wasn't sure when he had stopped looking forward to it.

And while Wally loved his family, he often felt as though he was walking through life on autopilot. The spark in his marriage was dimming, suffocated by the weight of bills, exhaustion, and unspoken frustration.

At the docks, Wally had found camaraderie with his co-workers—men who carried their own disappointments and dreams left unfulfilled. After long shifts, they often gathered at the local bar, swapping stories about better days and airing grievances about the present. Those nights soon became the only thing Wally looked forward to, the only space where he felt free from the weight of his responsibilities. But even those fleeting moments of escape came at a cost.

One sweltering afternoon, the phone at the docks rang—a rare occurrence for Wally. Kevin never called. He had only stopped by a couple of times since starting med school, and Wally couldn't recall a single time his best friend had actually phoned him.

Curious, Wally hurried to the office, where his manager was already eyeing him with disapproval. Personal calls weren't exactly encouraged on the clock. Ignoring the look, Wally grabbed the receiver.

"Hey, Kev, everything okay?" he asked, a note of concern creeping into his voice.

"Oh yeah, everything's groovy!" Kevin's voice crackled through the line, buzzing with excitement. "I just wanted to let you know I'll be in town tonight. Thought I'd swing by and catch up."

Wally relaxed, a small smile tugging at the corner of his mouth. "Yeah, sure, pal. Come on by."

"Great! Med school has been incredible! I can't wait to fill you in." Kevin said, his enthusiasm practically radiating through the phone.

A beat later, they said their goodbyes, and Wally hung up, ignoring his manager's lingering glare.

Kevin sounded excited, alive, like a man with the whole world ahead of him. Wally exhaled, running a hand through his hair before heading back to work. He was happy for Kevin. He really was.

Wally trudged back to his post, climbing into the crane and dropping into the seat with a sigh. He wiped the sweat from his brow, his calloused hands resting on the familiar, vibrating controls. Around him, the docks pulsed with life—the usual shouts of workers, the clang of metal, the distant crash of waves against the pier.

To anyone else, it was just another day. But to Wally, it was something else entirely—a reminder of everything he'd left behind.

He was supposed to be someone else. Someone bigger, brighter. A football star. A college graduate like Kevin.

Instead, he was here, a cog in the endless machine of dock work, his dreams buried under the weight of responsibilities he hadn't seen coming.

His shift had ended hours ago, but Wally couldn't bring himself to go home. Not yet. Home meant facing the quiet disappointment in Susan's eyes, the growing gap between them that neither of them seemed to know how to bridge. It also meant coming back to Susan, who would be just as worn out from her job. She hadn't planned to work—she'd always wanted another child—but once Mikey started school at the local community center, they couldn't afford for her to stay home.

Wally hated the look on her face, the one that seemed to accuse him of not providing enough. It left him raw, ashamed, and exhausted in a way that had nothing to do with hours spent hauling crates at the docks.

Going home meant facing the weight of fatherhood, a role Wally didn't feel equipped to fill. So instead, he lingered, watching shadows stretch across the pavement, delaying the inevitable just a little longer.

When James invited him to join the boys at the bar for a drink, as he often did, Wally didn't hesitate. One drink turned into two, then three, the hours slipping away faster than he realized. By the time he finally pushed back from the bar, his head was buzzing, and he knew he'd had more than he planned.

By the time Wally stumbled through the door of their small apartment, the air felt colder than usual. Quiet. Too quiet. The door creaked open, and he stood there for a moment, blinking to adjust his vision to the dim light. The only sounds were the soft hum of the radiator and the steady rhythm of Susan's breathing. She was already in bed, sound asleep.

The sight was both beautiful and heartbreaking. Susan's hair was slightly mussed, her face calm in sleep, but the unspoken heaviness in the room lingered like a shadow Wally couldn't shake. He swayed on his feet, watching her from the doorway, the weight of his exhaustion pressing into him like an anchor.

He took an unsteady step forward, the familiar creak of the floorboards beneath his boots pulling him further into the moment. As he bent to remove his boots, he stumbled, catching himself on the edge of the wall. His breath hitched, his eyes stinging.

"Where were you?" Susan's voice cut through the stillness, sharp and heavy with disappointment.

Wally blinked, his mind foggy but not entirely clouded by the drinks he'd had. "Just letting off some steam with James and the boys," he mumbled, his words slurring slightly as he leaned against the doorframe for support.

"You seem to be doing that a lot lately," Susan replied, flicking on the bedside lamp. The sudden glow illuminated her tired eyes and furrowed brow. "Every night, in fact."

Wally sighed, rubbing his temples. "It's been rough on the docks," he said, wobbling into the adjacent bathroom. He turned on the faucet and splashed cold water on his face, the icy sting bringing a moment of clarity.

Susan's voice followed him, quieter now but no less pointed. "When are you ever going to spend time with us? Your family?"

"I know. I know," Wally muttered, waving a dismissive hand as he emerged from the bathroom. "I promise I will. Tomorrow." He wanted to be a good father to Mikey—he really did. But there was so much life and stress in the way. He worked every day to provide for his family and wanted to give his son a good life, but it seemed like no matter how hard he tried, they were always barely making ends meet—even with Susan working part-time or full-time.

Susan turned to face him, her skepticism evident. "I've heard that before," she said softly, her words laced with exhaustion. She reached over and turned off the lamp, rolling onto her side and facing away from him.

Wally stood in the dim light of the hallway, the silence deafening. A hard pang of guilt hit him square in the chest, twisting his stomach into knots. He sank onto the edge of the bed, staring at the back of Susan's silhouette, her shoulders tense with frustration.

He knew he was failing her—failing all of them. His life felt like a runaway train, and he couldn't seem to find the brakes. But in his wake, he wasn't just wrecking himself—he was dragging his family down with him.

The next morning, Wally's one day off for the week, he sat slumped at the kitchen table nursing a cup of coffee. It was Saturday, and all he wanted was to relax, and maybe watch college football with his buddies. But Susan, already bustling around the apartment with Mikey, had other plans.

"We should take Mikey to the park—throw the ball around, have a picnic. You've been promising to teach him how to throw a spiral—he's been waiting," she said brightly. "It's a beautiful day, and we both have the day off. We could spend some time together as a family."

Wally sighed, rubbing a hand over his face. As much as he wanted to toss the ball around with his boy and spend time with Susan, his old leg injury might flare up—another reminder of better days on the football field.

"I just need one day, Susan. One day to unwind," he muttered. "I was thinking I'd watch the game with the fellas."

Her cheerful tone faltered, replaced with quiet frustration. "But last night, you said…"

"I know what I said. But I've got a nasty hangover and just need to decompress for a minute," Wally said. "Tomorrow, let's go to the park."

"Wally, it's Saturday. You're barely home as it is. Don't you think Mikey deserves some of your time too?"

The tension in the air thickened, the argument brewing

Living A Dream

before either of them could stop it. They both knew the script by now—her asking for more, him defending how little he had left to give.

Before they could go further, the doorbell rang, cutting through the moment. Wally frowned, glancing at the clock. It was too early for his buddies. He opened the door, and there stood Kevin.

Kevin looked like he'd stepped off a movie set. Dressed in a tailored coat, clean-shaven, with an effortless confidence that radiated from him, he looked every bit the successful man Wally once thought he'd be himself. His glasses gleamed in the daylight, his smile warm and easy.

"Kevin," Wally mumbled, blinking hard. Standing there, hungover and disheveled, he suddenly felt small.

Susan appeared behind Wally, her face lighting up at the sight of Kevin. "Hi, Kevin!" she said, stepping forward to hug him.

"Wally! Susan!" Kevin's voice was a mix of warmth and surprise. He turned to Susan and repeated what he told Wally over the phone. "I just got into town and thought I'd stop by and see you three."

"We're so glad you came!" Susan said, welcoming him inside with a warm smile.

Wally moved aside to let Kevin in, his stomach twisting as his friend's eyes swept over the apartment. Kevin didn't say anything, but Wally could see him taking it all in—the clutter of empty beer bottles on the counter, the stack of overdue bills on the table, the faint weariness etched into Susan's face.

"How are you both? How's Mikey?" Kevin asked, his tone warm but laced with genuine concern.

Wally ran a hand through his unkempt hair, leaning against the wall. "We're... surviving."

Susan, always the gracious one, quickly busied herself tidying up the beer bottles and bills, trying to make their modest home feel a little more presentable.

"Have a seat," Wally offered, gesturing to the couch.

Kevin sat quietly, his eyes scanning the room with his usual thoughtful curiosity. Susan returned a moment later, balancing a tray with a few colas, and handed one to Kevin.

"Thanks, Susan," he said with a polite smile, accepting the drink.

They had barely settled in when six-year-old Mikey came barreling into the room, his legs pumping furiously as he sang out "Yellow Submarine" at the top of his lungs. He ran in wild circles around the living room, his high-pitched voice echoing off the walls and making any attempt at conversation impossible.

"Hey, buddy!" Kevin grinned, leaning forward. "How's school going? Your mom tells me you're doing great. And how's Little League soccer? Scored any goals yet?"

Mikey's eyes lit up, and he launched into an excited explanation, words tumbling over each other. Kevin chuckled, listening intently, and then reached into the bag at his feet. "Got something for you," he said, pulling out a brand-new soccer ball—official size, with bright blue and white panels. "Figured you could use it for practice."

Mikey's jaw dropped, eyes wide with delight. "Wow! Thanks, Uncle Kevin!" he squealed, clutching the ball to his chest.

Wally forced a smile, but a knot tightened in his chest. He'd been meaning to get Mikey a new ball for weeks, but with money stretched so thin, it never made it to the top of the list.

"Take him back outside," Wally said, his tone sharper than he'd intended.

Susan froze for a moment, her expression clouding with frustration. She clearly wanted to stay and visit with their old friend, but instead, she took Mikey by the hand and led him toward the backdoor, her movements stiff.

"Come on, honey," she said, trying to keep her voice light.

Living A Dream

"Let's get you ready for soccer practice." She threw Wally a tight smile before disappearing out the back.

Once she was gone, Kevin shifted uncomfortably, breaking the silence. "So, I hear you've been picking up extra shifts at the docks."

"Yeah," Wally muttered, shrugging. "We're behind on bills, so I'm trying to catch up." He paused, then forced himself to ask, "How's med school treatin' ya? You said you had good news?"

Kevin's eyes brightened as he spoke, the excitement in his voice unmistakable. "Yes! We start hospital rotations in two weeks! I'll finally get to work alongside doctors and learn the tricks of the trade."

"Oh, that sounds like it'll be a great opportunity," Wally said, trying to sound happy for his friend.

"Man, I thought college was hard, but med school is on a whole new level. But, I've met so many new friends—everyone's sharp, you know? Real go-getters. I joined this med club, and we've been doing all these groovy events. It's like doors are swinging wide open, man." He leaned forward, his grin widening. "And one of my professors? He's the real deal, Wally. He got me into this program where we get to scope out surgeries. *Actual surgeries*, man. Last week, I watched a heart procedure up close. I was right there, seeing it all happen. Wild, right?"

The words hit Wally like a gut punch. Kevin's life was everything Wally had once envisioned for himself—full of energy, purpose, and possibility. Clubs, mentors, opportunities—Kevin had found his path, and it stretched out before him, limitless. Meanwhile, Wally couldn't see past the next day, trapped in a routine that felt less like a life and more like a slow, inescapable nightmare. Kevin kept talking, his voice electric with enthusiasm, but Wally could barely hear him now. He just stared at the table, his chest tightening with the sharp sting of envy.

"Sounds like you've got it all figured out," Wally said, his voice thick with barely concealed envy. He took a long sip of his cola. "Good for you."

Kevin's smile faltered slightly. "Hey, come on, man," he said, leaning forward. "You're doing something important too. Raising a family? That's no small thing."

Wally let out a hollow laugh. "Yeah? Tell that to the creditors. Or the landlord. Or... Susan."

Kevin's face softened with concern. "It's just a rough patch, Wally. You'll get through it."

"Will we?" Wally snapped, his temper rising. "I'm busting my ass at a dead-end job. Susan has to pick up day shifts at Giant Food while Mikey's at school just to help cover the bills, and I don't even know how to be a father. Hell, I don't even know how to be a husband anymore."

"You'll figure it out," Kevin said, trying to sound hopeful. "You always do."

Wally just shrugged.

Kevin studied him, the weight of his friend's despair settling heavily in the room. Finally, he stood, his voice soft. "I should go. But if you ever need anything—anything at all—I'm only a phone call away."

At the door, Kevin paused and turned back. "You've got a beautiful family. Don't forget that."

When the door clicked shut, Wally stood in the silence, the words echoing in his mind. He glanced toward the backyard, where Susan and Mikey kicked a soccer ball back and forth. They deserved better. They both did.

Quietly, Wally sank onto the couch, burying his face in his hands. He wanted to be the man Susan had fallen in love with. He wanted to be the father Mikey needed. But with every passing day of unrelenting work and expectations—and bills—that version of himself felt further and further out of reach.

Deep down, Wally couldn't help but wonder if that person

had been lost for years—and if there was any way to bring him back at all.

...

Wally took another bite of his sandwich, his gaze drifting to a family across the hospital cafeteria. A young boy—several years younger than Mikey—was mid-tantrum, his cries slicing through the low hum of conversation. Food scattered as he flung a fistful of fries, his mother's whispered pleas only fueling his defiance. Heads turned. Eyes narrowed. But Wally didn't join in their judgment. Instead, a faint smile tugged at his lips.

Mikey used to do that. His Mikey. Wally could almost see him—face flushed with stubborn determination, small hands clutching a toy he refused to give up. But as he tried to latch onto a specific memory, it split apart—two versions overlapping, blurring, slipping out of reach. Two kitchens. Two houses. Two lives that didn't fit together.

His grip tightened on the edge of the table. His breathing hitched. The cafeteria noise faded into a dull hum, drowned out by the dissonance tightening around him like a vise.

Wally shook his head sharply as if he could scatter the confusion like crumbs. What was happening to him? The memories weren't just fuzzy or distant—they were competing. Two versions, both vivid, both real. But they couldn't both be true.

The cafeteria noise surged back into focus, grounding him. Wally exhaled and looked down. His sandwich sat untouched. His appetite was gone.

...

. . .

The truth was, it hadn't been a good year—just one more bad year in a long string of bad years. Wally had been coming home later and later, finding reasons to stay out just a little longer, stretching the distance between him and Susan like a fraying rope. The long shifts on the docks drained him, and by the end of the day, all he wanted was to escape. A cold beer, a football match with his buddies—it was the only time he felt free.

But that freedom came at a cost. While he was out chasing that fleeting sense of relief, Susan was going from home to work and back again, taking care of Mikey and waiting. Waiting not just for him to walk through the door, but for him to show up—really show up—for her and for Mikey.

Mikey was six now, and Wally had missed too much. Too many bedtimes, too many milestones, too many of the little moments that Susan had been quietly collecting, like tiny heartbreaks she carried on her shoulders. She didn't say much at first, but Wally could sense her pulling away, brick by brick as if building a wall around herself to protect what was left of her hope.

Then came the Sunday morning when everything unraveled. Wally had promised—again—that they'd go out and spend time together as a family. But when his friends showed up at the house with six-packs of beer, ready to watch football, that promise slipped away. Within minutes, Wally and his friends were sprawled across the living room, beers in hand, the football game roaring from the television.

It was his sanctuary—the one place he could block out the weight of everything else. But clearly, Susan couldn't block out him and his empty promises anymore.

She stormed in, her voice slicing through the crackle of the game. "Get out of my house!" Susan's tone was firm, her glare unwavering as it swept over Wally's friends. Uneasy glances flickered between them before they mumbled their apologies and filed out, the door closing behind them with an awkward thud.

Wally turned to Susan, his frustration simmering just beneath the surface. "What the hell's your problem? You just embarrassed me in front of my friends!"

"Too bad," she shot back, her voice trembling but steady. "I'm tired of this, Wally. I'm tired of you. Mikey's six, and he barely knows his father. You're never here, and when you are, you're a ghost."

His anger flared. "Do you think I have time for this? I work my ass off to keep food on the table, Susan!"

"I know that!" she cried, her voice rising. "But why can't you be here for us when it actually matters? Why does it always have to be your friends, the bar, the game on TV? Mikey needs you, *we* need you, but you'd rather waste your time drinking and pretending you're single and childless!"

Her words were like kindling to his temper, feeding the fire roaring inside him. "I'm trying to change, I'm trying to be better, can't you see that? Why can't you accept that I'm trying and not nag the life out of me!"

"How, Wally? *How* have you changed?" Her voice cracked as she gestured to the empty beer bottles, the remnants of his good time. "You're still the same—coming home late, smelling like whiskey, disappearing every weekend. You promised me. You *swore* things would be different!"

Something snapped. It was like she was accusing him of being his father. And worse, he was terrified she might be right. All his fear and anxiety boiled over into rage. He grabbed the half-empty beer bottle from the table and hurled it against the wall. It shattered with a deafening crash, glass scattering across the floor like jagged stars.

Susan froze, her face pale, her breath caught in her throat. The silence that followed was heavier than any shouting could've been. For a moment, her eyes searched his face, hoping for regret. There was none. Only anger.

She took a sharp breath, steeling herself. "Come on, Mikey," she said, her voice low and tight. She turned to where Mikey stood frozen in the hallway, eyes wide and uncertain.

"Mikey, grab your shoes. We're leaving," she repeated, firmer this time. Mikey hesitated for a moment, then moved to the door, picking up his shoes. Susan was right behind him. And then, just like that, they were out the door.

"Susan, wait—"

"Goodbye, Wally." Her tone was icy and final. The door slammed behind her, and seconds later, the roar of the engine tore through the quiet, followed by the sharp screech of tires fading down the street.

Wally stood there, fists clenched, chest heaving. The house was too quiet now, his ears ringing from both the shouting and the silence left behind. His gaze drifted to the shards of glass glinting on the floor, then to the streaked beer running down the wall.

In the mirror above the hallway sink, he caught his reflection. A man stared back at him—wild-eyed, disheveled, fists still trembling. It wasn't Wally Masters. It was Boyd. His father. The same cold fury. The same vacant, drunken rage.

"Damn it," Wally muttered, his voice hoarse, barely a whisper. Before he could stop himself, his fist shot forward, connecting with the mirror. The glass splintered beneath his knuckles, cracks spiderwebbing outward until his reflection was nothing but fragments.

The house seemed to grow darker with every passing second. Wally grabbed another beer from the fridge. Then another. And another. Each one dulled the edges of his regret, at least for a little while.

By the time he passed out on the couch, the house was silent and empty. The shards of glass remained on the floor. The broken mirror hung like a wound on the wall. And Wally, sprawled and lifeless beneath a thin haze of alcohol, was alone.

...

Now, in the hospital cafeteria, Wally stared down at his plate, realizing he had shredded his sandwich into an unrecognizable mess. His stomach churned—not from hunger, but from the unease creeping under his skin.

The problem wasn't just the memory itself. It was the fact that he wasn't sure if it had even happened that way.

As vivid as it was, another version pushed forward, just as sharp, just as painful. Two conflicting accounts, both leading to the same outcome: Susan's anger, the rupture between them.

Which one was true?

Wally rubbed his temples, trying to steady himself, but the lines between memory, dream, and reality blurred until they disappeared altogether.

...

nine

...

WHILE JUGGLING the relentless demands of medical school, Wally was almost never home. His schedule was punishing—classes, labs, study groups, hospital rotations, and shadowing doctors at different hospitals. To help cover tuition, Susan took on a part-time job while Mikey was at school, and Wally picked up extra shifts at the university clinic, stretching his already thin reserves even further.

Most nights, by the time he made it home, Susan was already asleep—exhausted from her own day of work and taking care of Mikey. Most weekends, instead of spending time with his family, Wally found himself needing to blow off steam from the pressure of school.

That was how he ended up spending more and more time with a group of fellow med students and nursing students—people who understood the grind, the exhaustion, the constant push to excel. Among them was Deborah. She was a nursing student, sharp-witted and confident, with an easy charm that made stressful days a little lighter. Since med students and nursing students often crossed paths in shared classes and clinical activities, Wally saw her regularly.

At first, he kept his distance. He was careful not to cross

any lines, careful not to give Susan any reason to worry. But as the year wore on, he and Deborah became friends. She had a way of making even the most grueling days bearable, and though Wally never sought it out, it became clear that Deborah had taken a liking to him.

She started testing the waters—small comments, lingering glances, a touch on his arm that lasted just a second too long. At first, Wally brushed it off as harmless. But over time, he found himself looking forward to her company. He told himself it was nothing, that he was just enjoying the camaraderie of a colleague. But deep down, he knew there was more to it than that.

Everything came to a head during a Christmas party hosted by the medical faculty. The room was buzzing with music, laughter, and the warmth of holiday cheer. Wally stood with a drink in hand, chatting with his group, when Deborah sidled up to him. Her laughter was a little too loud, her hand resting casually on his arm as she leaned in to speak to him. Wally noticed the glances from the others, but he brushed them off.

Then, out of the corner of his eye, he saw Susan.

She stood across the room, her gaze locked on him, her expression unreadable. It wasn't until Deborah laughed again, flipping her hair and leaning closer, that Wally saw it—the fury flashing in Susan's eyes. She stormed across the room, her heels clicking against the polished floor, and slid her arm through Wally's.

"Hi, honey," she said sweetly, though her tone was laced with venom. Then she turned to Deborah with a tight smile. "And you are?"

Deborah blinked, startled, but recovered quickly. "Hi, I'm Deborah. Wally's told me so much about you."

"So interesting," Susan said coolly. "He's told me nothing about you." Her grip on Wally's arm tightened.

The tension was palpable, and Deborah quickly excused

herself, leaving Susan and Wally standing in silence. The car ride home was just as quiet, heavy with unspoken words. As soon as they paid the babysitter and the front door clicked shut, Susan rounded on him—arms crossed, her face hard with anger.

"You seem awfully close to that Deborah," she said, her tone sharp, each word deliberate. "I didn't see a ring on her finger."

Wally stiffened. "There's a lot of single people in my program. She flirts with everyone."

"Ah," Susan shot back, her voice like a whip. "So she does flirt with you."

"That's not what I said," Wally growled, his jaw tightening.

"What's going on between you two?"

"Going on?" Wally tossed his keys onto the counter with a sharp clink. "Nothing's going on. She's just a classmate. A colleague. That's it."

Susan folded her arms, her stance unwavering. "It sure looked like more than that."

"It's not," Wally snapped, his voice rising with frustration. "Just drop it."

But Susan didn't. "Tell me the truth," she said, her voice pressing into him like a knife.

"I *am* telling the truth." Wally turned on his heel, heading for the bedroom, his steps heavy with irritation.

Susan followed, undeterred. "Has anything ever… happened between you two?" Her voice softened, but the edge was still there, razor-sharp.

Wally froze for half a second, his back to her. The truth was, nothing had technically happened—but Deborah had been pushing the line for weeks. They had started to share small moments—an exchange of glances, subtle touches on the arm or hand, a familiarity that felt electric but also dangerous.

Living A Dream

He knew Susan had been feeling lonely like he didn't want to spend time with her. But with both of them so stressed and their lives so complicated, it seemed like they had stopped having fun together years ago. Every conversation felt heavy, every evening stretched tight with silence or exhausted small talk.

Wally's heart would flutter when Deborah entered the room, and while he had managed to keep things from crossing into outright betrayal, he could see the trajectory they were on. If it continued, he knew they'd cross lines they could never come back from.

But how could he explain all of that to Susan? How could he put those complicated, messy feelings into words without making everything worse?

His hesitation said everything Susan needed to hear. Her face twisted with hurt and anger. Then, at the same moment, they both heard a noise and turned.

Mikey stood in the hallway, worry and confusion written all over his face.

"Get your coat," Susan said, her voice tight. She grabbed hers from the hook by the door and hurried him outside without another word.

"Susan, wait—" Wally said, rushing after her.

But she wouldn't stop. She wouldn't even look at him. She opened the car door, buckled a very sleepy-eyed Mikey into his seat, and climbed in. With one last glare, she slammed the door, locked it, and sped off into the night.

Wally didn't know how long he stood there, staring at the empty road. Eventually, he went back inside, grabbed a cold beer from the fridge, and sank onto the living room sofa. Unable to process what had just happened, he stared at the floor between gulps.

...

. . .

Now, in the fluorescent glow of the hospital cafeteria, Wally stared blankly at the crumbs scattered across his tray. He didn't like this memory, either. The way it twisted in his gut, filling him with regret.

Sitting there, Wally wished for a third option. A version of the past where he hadn't let the distance between him and Susan widen into an unbridgeable chasm. A version where his choices hadn't fractured their family. But the past was a locked door, and no amount of regret could force it open. All he could do now was sit in the sterile hush of the hospital cafeteria and hope—hope that it wasn't too late to piece together what he'd broken.

Closing his eyes, Wally tried to untangle the knotted mess of his memories. He needed to know what was real, at least enough to know what he was supposed to apologize for. The hospital had fallen unusually still—as if the entire building, every nurse, every patient, had paused to take a breath. In that strange silence, Wally rose from his seat and wandered.

His steps were aimless, the halls blending into one another like a dream he couldn't wake from. He climbed stairs, descended others, and turned corners that led him nowhere, his feet carrying him without intention. Eventually, he stopped—somehow—at the grand piano in the hospital lobby.

Almost instinctively, Wally sank onto the bench, staring down at the black-and-white keys stretched out before him. But then his fingers hovered uncertainly. He knew how to play—didn't he?

In one set of memories, he did. He could see himself at a bench just like this, hands dancing effortlessly across the keys, his mother's voice guiding him through scales and songs. His father, the accomplished doctor, would nod in quiet approval from the doorway. In that life, Wally had gone to college and medical school. He had been living with the promise of a bright future—only to find his mistakes waiting for him. Mistakes named *Deborah*.

But in another set of memories, the keys were practically foreign objects. In that version, it was Kevin's mother who played the piano and Kevin's dad who was the doctor. Wally's own mother was the battered wife, and his father was the raging, broken man who wielded anger like a weapon.

In that life, Wally had never touched a piano. His dreams of college and glory had ended on a football field with the sharp snap of a bone. The rest was bars and dead-end jobs, nights of drinking, thrown beer bottles, and Susan walking out the door with Mikey in tow.

"Could the piano be the key to figuring out which memories are real?" Wally murmured aloud, his fingers tracing over the smooth black-and-white keys.

His fingers pressed down, and to his surprise, a melody began to take shape. It came unbidden, flowing from somewhere deep and familiar—notes he didn't remember learning, yet somehow knew by heart. His hands moved instinctively, the tune rising softly, then swelling into something haunting and beautiful. A mirror of his soul, the music was aching and tender.

The slightly untuned keys filled the vast lobby, each note echoing into the empty space. Wally closed his eyes, surrendering to the sound. He played as if no one was there to hear, as if the music could reach into the cracks inside him and hold them together. For the first time in what felt like years, the heaviness he'd carried began to lift. The sharp edges of regret dulled, and for a moment, he felt weightless.

The melody became a thread, tying together pieces of himself he thought he'd lost. He saw his mother, her patient hands guiding his small fingers across the ivory keys. He could almost hear Susan's laugh on a college Friday night, her head leaning on his shoulder as he played songs he'd written just for her. The music carried him further—into dusty barracks where his comrades clinked beer glasses, their voices loud and tuneless.

The song said everything Wally couldn't. It explained the ache in his chest better than words ever could. It gave shape to his grief, to his longing, to the love he hadn't known how to show. The pain was still there, but it made sense now—an old wound begging to heal. The song felt like the real him, maybe more real than either of the versions of himself. For the first time, he finally felt like he'd found himself.

As the melody played on, Wally could see a clear path to a brighter future—one with Susan and Mikey, and maybe even more children. Grandchildren, someday. He saw himself as a surgeon, saving children from all around the world. He pictured their home, full of love and life. It was everything he'd ever wanted, and for the first time, he could see exactly how to reach it.

As his fingers moved, Wally understood what he had to do. He couldn't rewrite the past, but he could fight for what remained. He would find a way to fix things with Susan—to earn her trust again, to be her husband for real, the husband she'd always wanted. He would prove to Mikey that he could be the father his son deserved.

He would stop running from the ruins of his life and start rebuilding—brick by fragile brick.

The final note hovered in the air, lingering like a sigh. Wally opened his eyes—and froze.

Susan was standing there.

Her face was streaked with tears, her lips trembling as she tried to speak. She covered her mouth, as though holding back a sob, her wide eyes locked on him. "How…?" she began, her voice breaking. "How did you do that?"

Wally blinked, caught off guard. He'd expected anger, maybe even indifference. But this—this was something else entirely. "Do what?"

"Play," she said, her voice barely above a whisper.

"I've always played," Wally replied, his brow furrowing in confusion.

Susan shook her head, her tears falling faster now. "No, you haven't." Her voice was raw, almost pleading. "Wally, you've never played the piano in your life. When did you learn?"

He stared at her, the words hitting him like a punch to the chest. "What are you talking about?" He searched her face for understanding. "I played for you—back in college. You used to sit beside me while I wrote songs for you. You loved it. Don't you remember?"

Susan's face twisted, her disbelief cutting through the air. "College? Wally, we never—what are you saying? You've never played the piano in front of me. Not once."

The world seemed to tilt slightly under Wally's feet. He shook his head, his voice trembling. "But, I just played the piano. I wrote that song. How could I do any of that just now?"

Susan stared at him, her eyes searching his face as though it might hold the answers. "That's what I'd like to know," she said softly, her voice hollow.

For a moment, they stood there in stunned silence, the

weight of the unspoken stretching between them. Then, finally, Susan asked, her voice tentative, "What was that song you played? It was beautiful."

Wally looked down at the keys, his hands still resting there as if the music might return. "I wrote it," he murmured, the words coming from somewhere deep and uncertain. "I wrote it for you."

Susan blinked, her tears glistening in the soft light.

"I know I've played it before, but this time when I played it, I could see everything. All my mistakes, all the times I let you and Mikey down." His voice cracked. "I'm gonna fix it, Suze. I promise. I'll make it all up to you. I'll end things with Deborah. I'll—"

"Deborah?" Susan's expression immediately soured, the fury from earlier slowly returning. "Who's Deborah?"

Wally opened his mouth to respond, but a sharp voice cut through the air.

"Mr. and Mrs. Masters!"

They both spun around as a nurse hurried toward them, her expression urgent but composed.

"Mikey is out of surgery," she reported briskly. "The doctor would like to see you now."

Susan gasped. "He's out?" Her voice cracked, a mixture of relief and fear spilling out.

For the moment, it seemed they were both spared the hard conversation about Deborah as they followed the nurse, their steps quick, anxious, and wordless. The melody Wally had played still echoed faintly in his mind, but now it was drowned by the thundering of his heartbeat.

When they reached the room, the doctor stood beside Mikey's bed, his expression calm but focused. Mikey lay still, his small chest rising and falling beneath a tangle of tubes and wires. His eyes were closed, his face pale.

The doctor looked up as they entered, immediately reading the worry etched on their faces. He wasted no time.

"Mr. and Mrs. Masters, Mikey's surgery was a success. He's stable now."

"Any complications during the procedure?" Wally asked quickly, his hand instinctively reaching for Mikey's chart. Before he could grab it, the doctor pulled it back with a firm but understanding nod.

"Hold on, Doctor," the surgeon said evenly. "Let me walk you through his status first."

"Any signs of post-op infection or bleeding?" Wally pressed, his voice tight.

"Wally!" Susan interjected sharply. "Stop pretending to be a doctor. Let the real doctor explain."

Wally's mouth opened, but the words caught in his throat. "But I am a…" he trailed off, uncertainty creeping back in. His knees felt weak, and he sank into the chair beside Susan, his heart pounding.

The doctor's tone was steady but kind. "There were no major complications. No signs of infection or unexpected bleeding," he assured them. "Vitals are stable, and the procedure went as planned."

Beside him, Susan let out a quiet sob of relief, pressing her hands to her face. Wally slipped an arm around her shoulders. To his surprise—and a flicker of quiet relief—she didn't pull away.

"We'll want to keep him here for a couple of days for observation," the doctor continued, "but so far, everything looks good. You can sit with him if you'd like."

They both moved to Mikey's bedside, reaching out to take his small hand. The quiet hum of machines filled the space between them. Susan gently stroked Mikey's fingers, her own trembling slightly.

Wally exhaled deeply, relief settling into his bones as he watched his son breathe steadily. One weight lifted. Now came the harder part. He gave Susan time, letting her absorb the moment, hoping that maybe—just maybe—the fragile calm would open a door between them.

Finally, Susan lifted her tear-streaked face and met Wally's gaze. "I still don't understand how you played that song on the piano."

Wally leaned back. He'd thought the music had been a breakthrough—a key to sorting out the chaos in his mind. But Susan's confusion left him unsettled. "Help me understand something," he said slowly. "I've been having… conflicting memories. I don't know what's true anymore."

Susan's brow furrowed. "What do you mean?"

Wally hesitated, trying to steady his thoughts. "Did I go to college?"

She blinked at him as if trying to decide whether he'd completely lost his mind. "What kind of question is that?"

"Just… please, answer me," he said softly.

Her frown deepened, but she relented. "No. You didn't go to college."

Wally swallowed hard.

"Wally, what is this?" Susan's voice sharpened with concern, but when he didn't respond she sighed. "Why are you asking me these things?"

He leaned back in his chair, staring blankly out the window as the setting sun cast long shadows across the room. "So that means you were never upset about Deborah…" he muttered, his voice trailing off.

Susan raised an eyebrow. "What was that?"

Wally's head snapped back to her. "Nothing," he said quickly.

Susan folded her arms, glaring at him with suspicion.

Wally lifted his hands in surrender. "It's nothing, I swear. There's just a lot I need to sort out still."

Susan studied him for a moment, clearly torn between disbelief and worry. "What's going on with you?" she asked finally, her voice softer but edged with unease. "First, you're giving medical advice like you're a doctor—advice that possibly saved Mikey's life. Then you're playing the piano like you've been doing it forever. And now this." She shook her head, her gaze sharp and searching. "What's happening to you, Wally?"

Wally sat up straighter, his hands fidgeting in his lap. "I need to tell you something," he said quietly, his voice unsteady. He hesitated, searching for the words. "That day you left..." He swallowed hard, his throat thick with emotion. "I hit rock bottom, Susan. I didn't know what to do with myself. I paced around the house like a madman, and then... I lost it. I punched the mirror in the bathroom. Shattered it. My hand was bleeding, but I didn't even care because I had just lost everything that ever mattered to me.

"I didn't recognize myself anymore," Wally continued, his voice raw. "All I could see was him—my father. The drunk who never wanted me. Who told me I was a mistake? Who beat me half to death when I was eight years old."

Susan's gaze softened but she still didn't say anything. Wally swallowed hard, feeling the shame of that moment wash over him again. "That night, I don't even remember falling asleep."

He paused, looking down at the floor before meeting her eyes again. "But I had this dream."

Susan's brows lifted, just a fraction.

"It must have been a dream, but it was so much more," Wally said, his voice steadier now, as though saying it aloud anchored him. "It was so vivid, Susan. So *real*. I was living this whole other life. I grew up with a family—a real family. A mom who taught me piano. A dad who showed me the beauty of medicine. I never had a career-ending injury, and I went to college on a football scholarship. And you were there, Susan. You were with me through all of it."

She eyed him curiously. "Go on," she whispered.

Encouraged, Wally took a small step closer. "We had

Mikey, just like we do now. But we figured things out. We applied for new scholarships and got into med school. I was studying medicine, and we made it work. Then we had more kids—two more. Timmy, this firecracker of a kid who was always running around causing mischief, and Rebecca… oh, Susan, Rebecca was… perfect. She was always singing and dancing around the house, filling it with so much light. She reminded me of you."

Susan blinked quickly, as though holding back tears. Her voice came out soft, almost incredulous. "I didn't know you even wanted more."

Wally smiled faintly, his voice growing steadier. "I didn't know either. At least the real me didn't know. But that other me, the one the dream showed me, he knew I always wanted more. We built this life together—a beautiful life. I became a surgeon. A good one. Families trusted me to save their children. People flew in from all over just for me to operate. And you were there through all of it, Susan. You were able to quit this job at Giant Food and finally do what you love. You were my anchor."

His excitement carried him to his feet, and he began pacing as if the dream still pulsed beneath his skin. "I could see it. Years from now, ours was a home filled with love and laughter. We took the kids to the park, to movies, to their games and recitals. Our house was alive with noise—happy noise. We weren't just surviving, Susan. We were *living*. And we were happy."

The room fell quiet as Wally's words lingered. He turned back to Susan just in time to see her hand lift to her mouth, her shoulders trembling slightly. For a moment, he thought she might pull away—walk out and leave the conversation unfinished. But she stayed.

"What do you think it means?" she whispered, her voice breaking.

Wally sat back down, leaning toward her. "I think it was

more than a dream, Susan," he said softly. "It was showing me the life we *could* have had. The life we always wanted. The life I've always wanted to give you. It showed me that we could still have it, even now."

Susan looked down, a tear slipping free as she wiped it away with shaking fingers.

Wally's voice grew gentler, steadier. "Listen, I know I've messed up. I know that better than anyone. But I want to fix this—I want to fix *us*. I don't want that dream to just be a story. I want to make it real."

For a long moment, silence hung between them. Susan sat still, her expression unreadable as she processed his words. Finally, she spoke, her voice quiet and unsure. "Wally… that dream of yours—it sounds wonderful. It sounds perfect. But…" She took a deep breath, her gaze flickering up to meet his. "None of that is real. We don't have that. And we can't."

"Yes, we can! I know we can just like I knew how to play that song or read that X-ray." Wally shot back to his feet, his urgency pouring into the space between them. He moved around the bed to stand in front of her, lowering himself to meet her eye level. Gently, he took her hands in his. "I don't know how long it'll take, or how hard it'll be. But I'll do whatever it takes, Susan. The dream showed me the way forward—showed me what's possible. We can have that life. I know we can."

Susan held his gaze, the faintest flicker of hope breaking through the doubt in her eyes. Her lips trembled into a small smile, one that seemed to soften the years of pain between them.

Sitting in Mikey's hospital room, Wally watched their son sleep peacefully, his small chest rising and falling with steady breaths. The soft beeping of the monitors and the occasional shuffle of nurses in the hallway had become strangely comforting—a reminder that their worst fears had passed. Mikey was safe.

Across the dimly lit room, Susan sat in a stiff hospital chair, arms folded. She had been silent for a long time, still processing everything. The weight of the past few days clung to them both, a mixture of exhaustion, relief, and the ghost of what could have been.

The cold, sterile air settled between them before Susan finally broke the silence.

"How did the dream end?" she asked, her voice barely above a whisper.

Wally exhaled slowly, his eyes distant, lost somewhere deep in memory. The faintest smile tugged at his lips.

"We grew old together."

ten

. . .

THE FIRE CRACKLED in the hearth, casting golden flickers of light across the warmly lit living room.

Wally blinked, the memory of that day in the hospital fading as he finished the story and found himself back in his real home—the scent of pine and cinnamon lingering in the air, the glow of the Christmas tree illuminating the eager faces surrounding him.

His grandchildren sat at his feet in a semi-circle, their wide eyes reflecting the flames dancing in the fireplace.

Kevin sat nearby, his wife nestled beside him, both of them as familiar as family.

For a long moment, silence filled the room. Then, a small voice broke through.

"Grandpa...but what about the X-ray? If you weren't a doctor yet, how did you know what you found in the X-ray? How did you know how to save Mikey?"

Wally hesitated, choosing his words carefully. "I'm not sure," he admitted slowly. "Maybe it was something I'd seen in a show once or something I overheard Kevin's dad mention about another child. Maybe it was just my subconscious forcing me to be what my family needed. Or maybe"—

his eyes lit up with a quiet wonder—"what I truly believe it to be was a miracle."

He paused, his gaze softening. "But whatever it was, it didn't just save Mikey's life. It saved mine too. It saved this family."

"So… all because of this dream, everything suddenly changed?"

"In a way," Wally nodded. "It helped me see what was possible."

"Was it hard?"

Wally nodded as he let out a slow breath, his eyes reflecting years of wisdom, of love, of loss.

"I almost lost everything."

"That was the night I stopped drinking. That was the night I finally chose to fight for something real."

He glanced toward Kevin, his oldest and dearest friend.

"And I didn't do it alone."

Kevin smiled, shaking his head. "You gave me a hell of a time, though."

Wally chuckled. "Kevin saved me more times than I can count. There were nights when I was ready to fall apart, when I nearly gave in... but he wouldn't let me."

Susan reached for Kevin's hand. "He was always there for us."

Kevin shrugged. "That's what friends are for, right?"

Wally's expression softened. "No, Kev. You were more than a friend. You were the brother I should have had."

A hush settled over the room.

One of Wally's grandchildren hesitated before asking, "But what about your two brothers, Grandpa? And your parents?"

The warmth in Wally's eyes flickered with something far away, something distant.

"My family grew apart," he admitted. "Roy spent most of his life in and out of prison. I never saw him again. Tommy moved to California. He still sends Christmas cards some-

Living A Dream

times, but we were never close. And my parents..." He exhaled. "They died in a car accident not long after Mikey recovered."

A long silence.

"Did they ever change?" one of the children asked quietly.

Wally hesitated, then shook his head. "No."

He let that truth settle in, let it rest where it belonged.

"But I did. I vowed I would never be like my father."

His grandchildren leaned in closer, their faces filled with wonder.

"So... what does it all mean?"

Wally's gaze swept over the people in the room—his children, his grandchildren, Susan, Kevin. His family.

"It means that you have a choice."

A hush fell over the room, every ear hanging on his words.

"Life can be a dream, if you choose it. If you fight for it. If you believe in it."

His voice softened.

"I had a dream of a perfect life, one that felt like it was out of reach. But in the end... I lived that dream."

A small smile played on his lips. "And so can you."

epilogue
. . .

WALLY PASSED AWAY SHORTLY after that Christmas.

He fought bravely, but in the end, cancer took him quietly, peacefully—his family by his side.

A few days later, on a crisp early spring morning, his loved ones gathered around his grave, light jackets draped over their shoulders, as the breeze whispered through the trees, rustling the tender green leaves.

They stood together in silence, hands clasped, hearts full.

And there, carved into the stone, were the words he had lived by—

DREAMS REALLY DO COME TRUE.

THE END.

Made in the USA
Monee, IL
02 April 2025